REBEL MOON

V. CASTRO

TITAN BOOKS

Rebel Moon Part One – A Child of Fire: The Official Novelization
Print edition ISBN: 9781803367316
E-book edition ISBN: 9781803367323

Published by Titan Books
A division of Titan Publishing Group Ltd
144 Southwark Street, London SE1 0UP
www.titanbooks.com

First edition: December 2023
10 9 8 7 6 5 4 3 2 1

A CIP catalogue record for this title is available from
the British Library.

Printed and bound in the United States.

ᚠ

Rebellion is not for the impulsive or fool-hardy.
It is for the truth seekers, the restless, the real
third-eye seers who believe the howls of the
soul create miracles. Rebels manifest change.
Now tell me, are you a rebel?

— King Heron from *Letters to My Children*

THE UNIVERSE IS AN EVER-UNFURLING TONGUE OF A GIANT, SALIVATING BEAST
seeking prey. Its black and smoky fur cloaks mysteries
incomprehensible to the human mind or eye, but not
to *The King's Gaze*. Nothing escaped its coveting, cold,
watchful glare. It moved quietly in low orbit amongst the
dozen moons surrounding its destination.

Admiral Atticus Noble walked along the corridors of
the grand citadel with priests and two of his Krypteian
guards. He had an unannounced appointment with King

Heron. Noble smirked at the title; "kings" on the outer worlds were mere administrators. King Heron stood in front of him with three of his advisors and guards.

"What a beautiful and prosperous city," Noble said as he gave King Heron a smile. Heron didn't match this gesture. He knew exactly why the admiral had landed in his dropship in the center of the main square. The Realm always made their presence known.

"Thank you. I know you didn't come all this way to give me compliments."

"No. I did not, sadly. It is actually a matter of grave importance. I have the responsibility of finding Devra and Darrian Bloodaxe from Shasu. It pained me to know they had been given sanctuary here. Now, I kindly ask you: hand them over. When you do so, I will leave as if I never set foot here in the first place."

King Heron held his ground. "I cannot. They are my guests. Your business with them is not mine."

Noble walked closer and his entourage of priests and Krypteian Guard followed. Heron didn't allow his fear to show. He had given his word to the Bloodaxes. That was final. Noble looked to the vaulted ceiling of the citadel and the stained glass filtering the sunlight. He clapped his leather-gloved hands together. He chuckled to himself with a thought only he could see and hear. "I will ask you one more time. Hand over the Bloodaxe rebels."

Heron didn't have to think about his answer. "Again, I respectfully decline."

Noble looked Heron in his eyes. In his cold, dark stare

that showed he possessed no soul, the real Noble emerged. "Very well. That is your choice."

"It is."

Noble nodded. "Until we meet again." He turned on his heels and walked out of the citadel back to his dropship.

King Heron's general leaned into his ear. "What are your wishes with this turn of events?"

"Tell the Bloodaxes to prepare themselves. They must be ready to flee."

The general gave him a short nod and left. Heron stood alone and wondered if he would ever meet Noble again. He hoped not.

The hangar on one of the sides of *The King's Gaze* opened for a single dropship to emerge and land on the planet below. Atticus Noble stood in silence as he watched the scenes from the city of Toa on a monitor. The flames were the same bright color as the sand. It would burn so ferociously that no amount of its vast jade waters could quell the fires. Cleansing heat. Everything bends to flame. All that history, hundreds of thousands of years of memory, becoming ash in a matter of hours. No one would ever see the magnificence of the stone city as it was originally created. Noble felt nothing for the loss or those who lay dead. Each corpse looked exactly like the next.

There is hurt, then there is pain and agony, followed by utter despair. Finally, we are met with waking death.

That is where peace is found, because nothing exists in the sphere of annihilation. There is no fight left. Noble knew this because he could not be more dead inside, and that gave him a sense of peace and direction.

He glanced back to the six priests mumbling prayers under their breath, behind their masks with red streaks below the eyes and old kingdom calligraphy across the mouth. Their decadent thick red robes and wide-brimmed hats embroidered in gold and white always emitted the scent of incense and smoke, as if the folds captured the aroma to remind everyone that the old religion demanded piety at all times. Skulls topped with gold spikes sat on each shoulder. Their presence was a representation of the sacred and the profane in the universe. He preferred his uniform and weapons to robes. The five-thousand-strong army awaiting his arrival would respond to metal before prayer. They saw more of death than God. Death had to be their sovereign.

Noble landed in the main plaza, reduced to rubble as he had instructed. When the dropship doors opened, the scent of burning wood, paper, and flesh hit his nostrils. It was a familiar scent. He led the way down the metal ramp with the priests trailing behind him like a blood-sodden cape. Before him stood his closest advisor, Cassius, who saluted him upon his approach but ignored the priests behind him. Also in Noble's entourage were two Krypteian guards, Felix and Balbus.

Noble's eyes scanned the oblivion that lay before him. Numerous bonfires leapt into the sky with books being cast inside as fuel. Their useless words finding a fitting end. Battered and bruised citizens kneeled in subservience, their magnificent sculptures and buildings that once rose toward the heavens now demolished to a state of humble ruin. Toa priestesses had their clothes torn off their bodies. They shivered in horrific anticipation as they watched their fellow priestesses being branded with a glowing red iron.

Noble continued toward Cassius until they stood face to face. "I see it is all going to plan here. Real obedience starts in the ashes. Well done. Where is the administrator of this world? Cassius, I would like a word with him." said Noble with his unshakable confidence. His sharp and hollow features resembled a mere mask of skin over bone and animated evil. His presence demanded to be acknowledged, like a predator with its lethal attributes on show. Fear is all you can feel when you see them up close. But running is futile because the predator's nature is to hunt.

Cassius remained stoic, one of the reasons Noble respected him above others. Nothing seemed to shock him. Cassius was a man who would never fall prey to some existential crisis. He knew his static place in the Imperium and had made peace with that. Following orders to the letter came easy for him. "He's near the citadel, sir. He still fights."

Noble despised misplaced heroics. It was a waste of time and energy. People should always know when to give up. "Hmm. Where is this citadel?"

Cassius pointed across the vast courtyard above the soldier's heads toward a crumbling tower burning brightly with dark smoke billowing high into the atmosphere. "Just there. As I said, not much longer before it all collapses."

Noble's eyes narrowed at the sight. "Good. And have we captured the siblings?"

Cassius's jaw clenched yet remained steadfast. "Sir, the administrator has orchestrated their escape. They have created this web of helpers in the universe to keep them fighting and out of our grasp."

Despite this not being what he wanted to hear, Noble appreciated Cassius wasn't the sniveling type. He always gave news to him straight and spoke plainly. He didn't hide from the stark truth.

"Another reason why we show no mercy here. How many got away?"

"We destroyed most of their ships and men. Devra Bloodaxe and her brother, in the chaos, were able to evade us with a handful of ships."

"Everyone thinks they can escape until fate finds them cowering and pleading for their wretched lives. Find this administrator, Heron. Hopefully still alive. I want those Bloodaxe bastard siblings sooner rather than later."

King Heron kept journals of the many trials and tribulations of his succession and his reign. He also wrote letters to his children for when they were older and needed advice about life. They would inherit this kingdom, but he also wanted them to inherit some of his wisdom. They would have to navigate through the politics of the Realm, which was not easy since the death of the king. In fact, he despised the Motherworld and what it stood for: greed, bloodshed, and coercion. That is why he extended help to the Bloodaxe cause.

He knew about Shasu, how the Motherworld made domestic issues worse when they meddled with violence. The alliance was almost untenable once Balisarius had taken over as Regent. Balisarius relished in his power, he had spread his cancer throughout the Realm, killing so many worlds and innumerable people with the disease of war. King Heron would do whatever he could to overthrow that tyrant.

Alone in his personal office in the citadel, Heron tucked away his letters and journals in a box made to withstand time and the elements. It fit in a small recess below his desk covered with an animal skin. Not even an hour after the Bloodaxes left, he felt inspired to write. Shouts and the sounds of vehicles made him look to the door as heavy footfalls ran past. As he walked out of his office, a shadow with a familiar shape passed the stained glass in the citadel, handcrafted a century before. Guards secured the citadel and ran to their posts. Those who worked there fled with terror in their eyes.

No one noticed him as he ran by. He was dressed in plain clothing that day, and all were more concerned with their own safety. He rushed to the main entrance, pushing past bodies and shouts. His eyes glazed over with darkness of the deepest abyss in the waters of the Biwa Sea when he saw three warships arriving in their airspace. But he had taken a side. He had to live with that.

With his own eyes, he saw the first blazing fireballs bombard the city before him. Alarms blared to a deafening volume as the ground shook. More guards poured into the citadel. One grabbed his arm, with the sigil of First Elite Lieutenant. "I have been looking for you. You must flee! I have sent a patrol to your residence. There was little warning of their approach, but we received a dispatch from the Bloodaxes. They were attacked deeper into space but got away."

"I need to get to my family."

"Yes, sir. I will have transport sent there immediately. If anything should happen, I will also have another sent here to the citadel."

"Thank you." Heron turned from the guard and began to run to his family. The residence was not far, because he wanted his children to see the day-to-day running of a kingdom, but it was far enough for them to be in grave danger if the Imperium soldiers got to them before he did.

When he arrived, Maia stood with their three children in the grand foyer decorated with fresh flowers and large oil paintings of their ancestors. Now they were knocked down as the residence shook under the shelling. Yet, she still looked regal. From behind her outer robe, he could see the tip of her large, sheathed blade. He loved her bravery. If he died, their kingdom would be in good hands with her leadership.

Clara and Calliope stood either side of their mother, with little Clara holding the family pet, Bergen, in a small cage. The two girls shared their mother's fear. His teenage son, Aris, huddled next to his mother and sisters with a rifle in hand. He did his best to stay calm, but Heron knew his son was panicking inside. That was okay. With the direction the Motherworld was headed, he knew his children would experience war sooner or later. The Realm was unceasingly bloodthirsty, their senseless lust for violence never satiated. The destruction around him proved he was right to help the Bloodaxes.

"Heron, what is going on?" asked Maia.

"No time to explain now. Transport should be waiting outside. We go right now. Don't take anything but what you have on you." The walls of their home continued to crumble, the bombardment escalating. Shouts could be heard coming from the hallway that joined the foyer and the main sitting room. Heron snatched the rifle from his son, raised it above their heads, and pulled the trigger. Blood sprayed into the air, causing the little girls to scream.

He gave the rifle back to Aris then reached for Clara's hand to lead them out of the royal residence. The little girl took her father's hand. They ran through the front entrance into the unfolding devastation outside. Heron handed Clara to her sister and picked up a rifle that had been discarded on the ground. Through the smoke of burning buildings, they could see one of their own dropships approaching to land on the manicured lawn, surrounded by large palm trees to give the residence another shield besides the ornate high steel gates topped with spikes that looked like the open beak of a bird.

Soldiers and citizens ran outside the gates to escape the carnage. As the family looked to the sky, the dropship burst into flames. Maia gasped, "No."

A larger Imperium ship's shadow could be seen moving across the lawn of the residence. Heron and his family looked back. They were going to destroy their home. Cannon fire crashed not far from their feet. They all ducked from the spewed dirt and blood. Flesh flew across them. "To the citadel!" he shouted as he scooped Clara into his arms and began to run. The family dashed through the small side gate that was usually manned by elite soldiers outside. Heron looked into the retina lock. The steel gate opened.

Some of their soldiers lay dead, the others probably drawn out to the fight. When they passed the pedestrianized walkway between the residence and the path to the citadel, a large explosion made them duck and look behind them. The royal residence no longer existed. King Heron grabbed his son's arm and brought him close. "Beneath the floorboards of my office in the citadel are letters for you and your sisters. Your mother and Calliope know. If anything should happen—"

Another explosion stopped Heron from finishing his thought. He turned to run again toward an already bombarded citadel. It was their only remaining hope for escape. It was clear the Realm held no room for discussion or dissension. They wanted a homogeneous kingdom of ethnic purity and singular thought.

King Heron and his family crouched behind the fallen statue of a god who must not exist, because this place was devoid of any benevolence. His daughters, Clara and Calliope, tried their best to not cough from the choking smoke stinging their throats. Sweat rolled down his face and soaked his black tunic. He wiped his palms against his trousers to take aim at the soldiers who cornered them at the citadel.

His son still held a rifle. They all had to fight to make it out alive. His wife, Maia, and two girls moved through the giant shards of stone as Heron took aim. He landed a clean shot straight into the forehead of one of the soldiers. Crimson droplets sprayed into the air with the glowing embers carried on the wind from the razed city outside. He could hear Clara scream at the sight while Calliope impatiently shushed her.

But this is where Heron excelled, the part of him his daughters didn't know. Don't come for an expert marksman without expecting there is a chance you might land directly in their crosshairs. Soldier after soldier fell to the ground in rapid succession. His eyes scanned ten men through the smoke and gunfire. Despite his hits, more soldiers closed in with the movement of a vicious tide. He whipped his head toward his son. "We need to drop back."

His son didn't move. "But Father…"

Maia grabbed her son's forearm with a firm hold and stern, authoritative expression. She also glanced at her daughters. "You heard your father. We need to move. Girls, let's go now. To the door."

Heron nodded and his son obeyed. They made their way to the stairs. Bergen squawked in its cage as they moved fast. Calliope tried to make Clara part with it when the fighting began, but it was the only way Clara, at eight years old, would leave their home as their mansion took the first of the series of bombardments. It was a gift from her father. He had one when he was her age, his pet was Bergen's mother. The hairless blue creature was agitated, showing its tiny razor teeth and banged against its gilded cage. It's three-fingered grip pulled at the small opening, which was locked. "Shhhh, Bergen," she told the creature.

Her older sister, Calliope, pushed past hurriedly with a scowl on her face. "That thing is going to get us killed."

Calliope screamed and stopped as six soldiers approached the stairs. One grabbed her tightly with both his arms over the top half of her chest. She struggled and kicked, but he was too large for her to escape. Clara began to holler and cry. Bergen mimicked her with a screech. Heron rushed behind Clara and took aim just above Calliope's head. She knew to stay still and stopped trying to fight back. In an instant, her captor's blood jetted across her face and hair.

Heron dispatched the rest of the soldiers. Out of the soldier's clutches, Calliope ran to her father, who continued up the stairs, rifle at the ready for whoever stood in their way. The family sprinted with the soldiers cleared away. Maia led with the girls. Another scream rang through the stairway. It was his wife.

Heron bolted as fast as he could, ignoring his aching muscles and dry mouth. He saw Maia plunging her wedding gift, a twelve-inch engraved curved blade dripping in blood, into the neck of an attacking soldier. Another rushed toward her. This one got it in the stomach. A powerful, sure slash that split him open.

Her hand trembled, wrapped around the smooth wooden handle decorated with gold. When they had no choice but to leave their palace, she tucked it into a belted sheath beneath her robes. The blood of the soldiers had painted her face and gown. The moment of pause was interrupted by a series of loud beeps followed by an explosion of stone and dust. The stairs and columns behind them were deliberately destroyed.

Heron and his son ran for cover beneath the fortified archway as the stairway behind was damaged. Maia and the two girls were thankfully already safe inside the throne room in front of them. Their hair and skin were covered in powdery debris clinging to sweat. Maia looked to the stairway and back at Heron with tears in her eyes. He knew her well enough to know the terror behind the tears she would try to hold back for the sake of her children. Every explosion and bullet blasted another hole in her heart, and the hope they would make it out alive.

Heron touched his son's shoulder. "Son, get your mother and your sisters to the throne room. Go."

The boy, bordering on early manhood, squeezed the barrel of the rifle in his hands and nodded. With a swift jerk he grabbed his youngest sister by her left arm. The sudden movement caused her to drop her unsettled pet. "Bergen!" she screamed.

"No! We must go. It will only slow us down," said Calliope.

Maia touched the back of Clara's head and took Calliope's hand. She looked back one last time at her husband with tears falling down her cheeks. The little creature pushed against the overturned cage to escape. No luck.

Heron turned to the sound of soldiers climbing over the rubble on the stairway. He aimed his rifle. A volley of shots hit all around him, blasting stone. There was little to no cover to be had as he tried to avoid them. He roared in pain and grit his teeth as a round hit his left thigh. He looked down at his torn flesh and pressed on the wound. Allowing only a moment to recover, he continued to fire at the soldiers until his rifle shot its final round. He glanced at the weapon and dashed around a remaining column. He flipped it around and waited for the next body to find his wrath.

His rifle wasn't completely useless. As a soldier approached, Heron smashed the butt into the center of his face. The soldier fell back with his nose dislodged and hemorrhaging blood. Six other men charged toward

Heron. His eyes darted, sizing them up. Forgetting his wound in the heat of battle, he fought his way through them with the ferocity of a wild beast taken with madness. He was not a beast or a king, but a father and husband fighting for the survival of his family.

He grabbed the soldier whose nose he had broken and used him as a shield as a shot was fired his way. Blood splashed Heron's face and mouth. His left hand grabbed the dead soldier's weapon before it could fall out of his hand and shot back, hitting the sniper through the neck. The five living soldiers walked through their fallen comrade's mist of blood as they unloaded their weapons at Heron, their bullets missing or wasted on the corpse shield. He fell to one knee and aimed with precision, fatally hitting three more before crawling behind a fallen statue. He glanced at the weapon. He would be out of ammunition soon. The next few shots had to count to kill the remaining two soldiers.

To his left he noticed a steel bar that had fallen from the destroyed statue. He grabbed it as a piece of insurance in the event his ammo ran out before he killed the soldiers. The footfalls were close.

"Over there!" he heard one of them shout. Heron inched his way up and discharged the remaining shots. He hit one in the face before his weapon died. He ducked down again, grabbed the bar, and waited for the soldier to reload. The shooting stopped and Heron met the moment. His body tensed in agony from his wounds as he crouched and lifted the bar at an angle. As the soldier ran to face Heron, he plunged the steel bar through his belly. The soldier dropped his weapon with wide eyes as he reached for the bar. Heron scrambled for the gun and shot the soldier until it ran out of ammunition.

His chest heaved as he looked at the dead soldier skewered on the steel bar. He winced at the pain emanating from his thigh. The length of his trousers sodden, crimson. His eyes glanced toward the stairs. A man whose uniform let him know he held the position of sergeant stood with a small army behind him, at least thirty soldiers. They had slight smiles from the amusement of watching the fight.

Heron's face dropped before running toward the archway. In the rush he tripped over a dead soldier's boot. He gathered himself from the throbbing pain and exhaustion of the fight. He saw Bergen. His memories of childhood and the joy in his daughter's eyes when she played with it flashed in his mind. It gave him hope. The creature trembled. He snatched the cage from the ground and crawled behind a large portion of fallen stone wall. With care, he opened the cage. He could feel the heat already building inside it as he gingerly removed it. The creature whined and squawked at being handled. He cradled it in one hand and rested his forehead against the creature's head, and whispered, "They want to hurt her."

The sound of his voice and breath calmed it down. With a blood-smeared thumb, he rubbed its belly. A deep hue of red began to glow from its insides. All its internal organs could be seen as they shifted. Heron continued to hold it close as it glowed brighter. The black threads of its veins became more prominent the brighter it became. "I wish it were me," he whispered as he opened his eyes and placed the glowing creature down. Its neck lolled as it balanced on its spindly hind legs before dropping to all fours. With its twig-like arms and padded hands, it scampered in the direction of the soldiers.

Heron watched with deep sorrow as it crawled with remarkable agility through the debris with its inner light cast across the floor like a roving beacon. Hope in the darkness. It had to exist. That flame had to be kept alive before the Realm snuffed it out with its breath stinking of gore and indiscriminate doling out of death. He closed his eyes, before using the last of his strength to raise his body from the ground. He groaned as he attempted to run after his fall. All he could manage was a quick limp.

"There!" a soldier cried out, aiming his weapon at Heron.

The sergeant whipped his head in Heron's direction. "Finish him," he commanded the private. Without any hesitation, the soldier lifted his weapon and aimed at his moving target. With his finger on the trigger, he noticed in his periphery a red light moving across the floor. He released the tension on the trigger and shifted his eyes from Heron to his feet. His brow furrowed upon the sight of some sort of creature. It lifted its trembling body upright with strained and ear-piercing cries as it swayed.

The sergeant's eyes widened upon seeing the shrieking animal growing brighter by the second with its dark veins pulsating in increasing speed. He said with a sneer, "No…"

In the next instant the room filled with an explosion to rival a grenade. The creature combusted with a force that vaporized the remaining soldiers. Heron had crawled far enough away not to meet the same fate; he was thrown face first to the ground from the impact. He lifted his head and coughed from inhaled dust and ash. With a deep groan, he reared his head and looked back. No survivors.

He had to find his family. Running was no longer an option, they'd have to hide until the invaders grew bored of attacking rubble. Heron limped into the throne room. Aris spotted him and waved for him to join them behind a fallen wall. "What do we do now, Father?" Aris asked.

Heron held onto his son's shoulder and lowered himself to the floor. He winced in pain and touched his wound. "We wait. Let them be satisfied they made a lesson out of us, then leave. We will rebuild. What is the point of hunting us down? But seeing this. This is why I had to do what I did. This type of power… force of will on another. It must be questioned."

He looked at his three children with love. "Promise me you will always ask questions and stand up for what you know is right." His family surrounded him and gave him a warm embrace with tears in their eyes.

Noble had to admit the citadel was an impressive structure, with three intervals of steps leading to the throne room.

He passed the entrance into the only remaining part of the once great building. Nothing existed except the echo of his boots amidst the destruction. To avoid soiling the leather, he weaved around the bullet-riddled and burnt bodies of the Inner Sanctum bodyguards that dotted the floor. It was a throne to ruin, with ash falling with the softness of snow. Next to him were Felix and Balbus, two of his best in the Krypteian Guard. The savagery of war permeated every crease and pore on their faces. It was enough to make some surrender in an instant. The original guards were plucked from a world that valued the same warrior mentality as the Motherworld. Their people knew how to fight, and fight hard.

Without any effort, Noble found the man he searched for, and as a bonus, his family. King Heron. They tried to remain quiet, huddled together like mice amongst the broken shards of stained glass and fallen stone as he approached. Two young girls' eyes quivered in fear as Noble approached. The youngest gripped her mother's arm and hid her face halfway behind her torso. He wasn't surprised.

The lead priest held the Golden Scepter, a femur gilded in gold and blessed with the ancient language etched in the metal. Behind him, one of the faceless priests breathing heavily behind their masks held an icon. It was the assassinated Princess Issa's image in a pure gold frame. Human teeth, rows of them, faced her image as if they bowed in pious service. To anyone, much less an ignorant child, it had to be frightening.

The ash continued to fall like small worms, maggots on rot. Noble brushed it off his shoulders with burning embers also blistering the atmosphere. His uniform could not be tarnished. The city outside would continue to burn for at least another day. When he stood before the family, he bowed, then returned to his imposing stance.

He watched the woman grab hold of both girls tightly then look at her husband. Heron sized up the guards and the priests. Noble knew men; if this one had any fight left within, he would attempt to kill them all for the sake of his young family and in the name of honor. But a single tear fell from the woman's cheek as she looked at her husband.

"Tell me, what are you thinking as you look at him that way? I genuinely want to know," said Noble.

She didn't speak straight away, visibly startled by his voice and the odd question. "I... just a memory of the first snow of the season. We were at our winter palace. It was... beautiful. The joy."

Noble swiveled his head toward Heron. "It saddens me, truly it does. It is a shame you are now cowering in ash rather than playing in snow. All of it is just so unnecessary... so utterly unnecessary. You made a choice."

He raised his leather-gloved hands, palms up, as if he offered them an alternative if only they would take his hands. Heron's face hardened, knowing he offered nothing and toyed with them.

"Please tell me your names."

The man straightened his posture. "King Heron, as you damn well know. This is Aris, my son, Maia, my wife, and my daughters, Calliope and Clara."

Heron placed a hand on his son's forearm. "Don't torture us. If you've come to kill me, do it. It was my decision to let them stay here and mine to help them flee. But for God's sake, please I beg you, let my wife and children live. They're innocent in all this."

Noble's eyes glided over the family, devoid of any emotion. There was only pure calculation. "Oh, I have not come to kill you. As a matter of fact, I come to assure you that your bloodline will survive, thrive. You fought with such dignity. How could I possibly kill you? However, there is a price to be paid, for your... shall we call it... your defiance. A price indeed."

Noble took a step closer to Maia. He searched her face before his eyes traveled to her neck and three open buttons on her dress. A teardrop fell on her collarbone. He looked back into her eyes and smiled. The calm in his expression could not mask the coldness in his eyes. The tip of his index finger caught a tear on her cheek. He looked at it as if it was a foreign object he would never understand. He moved on and fixed on Calliope, then Clara. The youngest one shirked from his towering frame. "Oh, so young," he said in a sinister tone before moving toward Aris, then stopping. "Stand up, let's have a look at you."

Aris remained still with a pensive expression as he looked at the armored Krypteian Guards sneering. Felix tapped on the trigger of his gun. Aris looked to his mother, who looked at him hard and shook her head in a slow, measured motion.

Noble's face twisted in anger. "I said, 'stand up'."

Aris moved closer. Clara whined, "No, don't." She tugged at his clothing, trying to hold him down. Understanding that every move away from her, toward Noble, was a move that could not be retracted.

Noble's eyes darted toward her with a sharpness that caused her to shrink further into her mother. "That a boy," he said as he placed a hand on the back of Aris's neck with his thumb and index finger digging deep to apply enough pressure to keep the boy under his control. Noble guided him away from his family, toward the two guards. Through gritted teeth, he whispered to him in a calm, low tone.

"There comes a point in every young man's life when he finds himself on the threshold of manhood. A moment he always remembers. A moment, that after, he can look back on and know from that moment on, he was a man. For some, it comes in the form of moist lips and full breasts of a woman. For others, it could be leaving home for the first time, striking out on your own. But for you, it will be a choice you made."

Noble twisted Aris to face his family and drew his lips close to his ear. "Are you ready to be a man? Your moment has arrived. Just like your father made choices against the Realm to bring us to this moment."

A priest took a step forward and raised the Golden Scepter toward Noble, who gripped the gilded bone with one hand.

"You see, I was charged by the Regent himself. He

looked in my eyes and bid me, bring to justice the siblings, Devra and Darrian Bloodaxe for their crimes of treason and insurrection. My search brought me here, where I learned your father had given them sanctuary and a base of operations from which they attacked and destroyed several assets belonging to the Realm."

"Why are you doing this?" pleaded Heron.

Noble's gaze snapped to Heron. He gently tapped the Golden Scepter on Aris's chest. "It's important your boy understand… What is his name?" Noble looked into Aris's tear-filled eyes. "What's your name, boy?"

Aris looked at the scepter, then back to his family, who all had dusty, weary faces with tear tracks running down their cheeks.

"Aris."

Noble cocked his head toward him. "I didn't quite get…"

"Aris!" he shouted back. His name echoed louder than the word "boy."

Noble narrowed his eyes and gave him a sly smile. "Good. Okay, Aris. Let's see if your father can't teach you one last lesson. Take this holy object."

Aris swallowed hard and took it into his shaky hands. The weight of it tugged at his arm for a moment when he first felt the weight of it.

"It is heavy. But that is what being grown sometimes means," quipped Noble. "Here is your choice. If you bash in your father's skull—I mean really bash it in until his brains spill out, on what was once this beautiful floor."

Noble strode over to Heron and knocked with his fist on his shaved head. He turned back to Aris. "I will let your mother and sisters live. But if you say 'no' like your father did... then you all shall die."

The only sounds were those of the destruction occurring in the city and the wails of the citizens in the distance. Aris searched the faces of his family for answers, for a way out. There was no reassurance. He looked at Noble; Noble looked back. His stare unrelenting and dead. But it was in the eyes of the Krypteian that he gained the final clarity, and his last sliver of hope died. In those eyes he saw no sympathy, nor relish, just an understanding of the current reality. Finally, his father spoke.

"Aris, listen to me. You need to do as he says. Save your mother and sisters."

Maia screamed from the depths of her belly with tears falling from her eyes, "Aris, no!" Clara and Calliope whimpered and cried. Heron looked at them frantically and back at Aris. He wiped the sweat from his forehead with the back of his hand.

"Don't listen to her. Don't look at her. Look at me. Save them. I am already dead."

Both girls began to cry into the dirty robes of their mother. Maia shook her head. "Aris, let us go... Let us all go. I can't live with this, and you can't either. You won't come back from this. None of us will. Please don't do this."

Heron shot Maia a stern look. "Don't you dare look at her, you stay with me!" he shouted as Aris continued to glance back at his mother and sisters. "I said don't look at her! Now, you do this. Be a man and do it. Save them. Do it. You are strong. Now save them."

Aris looked down at the scepter and squeezed it with both hands. He shut his eyes as if to divine the right course of action. Noble placed a hand on his. "Listen to your father, Aris. He is a wise man."

Aris opened his eyes again and raised the heavy relic. His eyes darted toward his little sister, who shook her head and cried in terror, while their mother sobbed with angry tears streaming down her cheeks.

"That's right, son. You need to listen to me… Now, do it." Heron said, before closing his own eyes. "I love you son… I forgive you."

In one swift movement and with all his young might, Aris plunged the scepter into his father's forehead with a scream that echoed through the emptiness of the ruins. Noble gasped as he sucked in air, as if he didn't truly believe the boy had it in him to follow his orders.

Maia clutched her children tighter with stifled sobs as she looked away. Clara and Calliope squeezed their mother's robe as they sobbed with her hands over their eyes. Felix and Balbus chuckled as Heron's eyes rolled behind his head as his body collapsed to the ground.

"Finish it," hissed Noble. He balled both his leather-gloved hands into fists.

Aris grit his teeth with tears and snot wetting his face. He raised the bone again and hit the crown of his father's head. This time with a crack tearing into the air as the skin split open and blood slowly seeped out. Aris raised the bone once more.

"I said I wanted his head wide open!" Noble placed both hands on Aris's rising and falling shoulders and squeezed.

Aris pulled away from Noble and heaved the scepter overhead. He thrust it into the back of his father's skull. And then he did it again, until blood and pulpy brain tissue splattered the floor. The crown of his skull was broken into shards. Heron's face was now unrecognizable, with his jaw dislodged and both eyes popped out of the sockets. He looked back to his mother, who had her hands over his sister's eyes. Both of them covered their ears with their little hands.

The collar of his tunic clung to his neck, wet with sweat, as he breathed heavily from the exertion. He stumbled back and tossed the relic at the feet of the lead priest. His chest continued to hitch as he fell to his knees. He looked toward the broken stained-glass window that would never be put together again. There was no one left to do it. The sunrise pulled illumination into the room. Blades of light cut across the floor, showing the horrific scene of a family broken.

Noble kneeled between Heron's body and Aris. One finger at a time, Noble removed his left leather glove with his teeth. He reached for a patch of Heron's blood-matted hair and lifted it to expose the rest of the open skull. "Hmm. Impressive, young man. You have a lot to learn, but this is a good starting point."

The sound of Maia and the two girls crying broke his inspection of the corpse. He lifted his gaze. "Rest assured, your son will thrive. It will be hard at first, but that anger and that sadness, that dead soul that's inside of him now, I can use all that. He can let his rage out, and he will, because as we track down those traitors you sacrificed everything for, and we will track them down, there will be so many proud rulers standing my way. So... he won't have long to wait."

Noble looked back at the growing pool of blood and smashed brain matter. He scooped a large chunk between his finger and thumb then brought it to eye level. His brow creased as he inspected it before grinding it to smaller pulp.

"That is the time you and he made love in the shadow of the Banyan tree in the warm summer grass. That was the time he cried at the birth of your daughter, and that, a moment no one saw but him... you sleeping. He brushed the hair from your eyes and kissed your forehead." He let the flesh fall from his fingertips. His eyes shifted to Maia, and he brought his bloody index finger to his temple and tapped it. "You see, it all begins here and is stored here. Destroy this enough and there is nothing left."

Maia's nostrils flared as her breathing increased. "You are an evil man."

Noble stood as one of the priests shuffled behind him and kneeled next to Heron's body. He held out metal pliers and pulled a single tooth from Heron's cracked jaw. The priest took the tooth and placed it amongst the other teeth surrounding the image of the princess.

Noble watched Maia's reaction before turning to Balbus and Felix. Both guards gave him a short nod. Felix yanked Aris off the floor and twisted him toward the entrance. "Get up. You are with us now."

Aris attempted to look back, but both guards pulled him harder by the armpits, dragging him to the still-burning inferno that was Toa.

The chanting of the priests increased as the light and heat of the rising sun filled the room. Noble turned back to Maia and her crying daughters. His eyes searched the ground until he saw the blood-soaked scepter. He bent down and picked it up.

"These games don't become you," said a defiant Maia.

Noble scraped brain and blood from the scepter with his bare hand. "Oh, how so?"

Maia wiped her tears with the back of her hand and straightened her posture. "The theater, the drama. It seems false on you. You're a man of action. You're not going to let us live. There can be no hope in some slave princess if the destruction of this world is to be complete."

Noble stepped closer to her, his eyes narrowed as he began to lift the scepter above Maia and her two daughters.

She snarled, "There you go. The honest soldier. There is no honor in you."

"No. There is not," said Noble as he swung the metal femur. He didn't stop beating the life out of all three of them until he couldn't see from their blood clouding his sight.

The two Krypteian guards escorted Aris out of the citadel and into the still-smoldering streets. A young woman lay on a fallen pillar with her dress torn from the chest and blood running down both legs, dripping to the ground from her toes. Her eyes were beaten shut. Felix laughed at the sight. "That will teach this world and hopefully more." Aris couldn't look, wouldn't. That could easily be one of his sisters, or mother. His father always taught him to respect others, and himself. Everyone, in the universe full of all sorts of creatures, genders, and humanoids, deserved respect. Dignity had to have some value still.

Aris wanted to look back to see if his mother and sisters would emerge, but he didn't have the energy. All he felt was numbness. He couldn't know for certain they were alright, and he did the right thing. Balbus wrenched his face forward. "This way, *soldier*. That is none of your concern now."

Aris kept his eyes on the glowing horizon that went in and out of focus. He couldn't believe the only place he had ever lived no longer existed. His father's and grandfather's kingdom gone. Dust and ash blew into his face, causing him to choke and cough. Felix grunted to Balbus, "He better get used to it. This is how we live and breathe. I wasn't much older than him when I started with the guard at the Krypteian Gauntlet for training. It was an honor." Felix beat his fist against his chest.

"He's way too soft, being raised here. This isn't Krypt.

Not a sprout of hair above his lip, and doubt he has any on his balls," said Balbus.

Both Felix and Balbus erupted into callous laughter. Then Balbus turned serious. "There aren't many of us left. We are a dying breed. Shame that the Guard, at least what it used to be, no longer exists." Felix nodded and grunted. Aris didn't speak, he couldn't on the matter. They approached a dropship that still seemed imposing to Aris.

Standing on the ramp was a man not dressed in armor, but a uniform. He didn't seem to have been in the heat of battle, perhaps an officer under Noble. His eyes ran the length of Aris's body but didn't seem surprised by his presence. In fact, there was little emotion. Aris couldn't get a read on him because he didn't seem to relish war like Noble or the guards, yet he didn't seem to have any pity either.

His father used to say sometimes the most dangerous men in times of peril are the ones who just go along with whatever bloody tide comes along. Aris wondered if this officer had got tied up with the Realm the same way he found himself now, and eventually gave up fighting it.

"Where is Admiral Noble?" the officer asked.

Balbus smirked. "Commander Cassius, he is tying up loose ends with the king. You know how he is. What is that saying? *Every child screaming, every mother crying.*"

Cassius looked to the distance. "Yes, that is correct. Very well. Get this boy on board. We have a schedule." As Aris was about to pass him, Cassius grabbed his arm. "What is your name?"

"Aris."

He studied him for a moment. "You will do exactly as I tell you, when I tell you. The Imperium demands loyalty without question." He let his arm go and returned to looking toward the burning citadel.

"May I ask where you are taking me?" asked Aris.

Cassius's eyes always appeared dead when first met; now, they darkened. "You belong to the Imperium now. You will train to be a soldier, boots on the ground. Stripped of your title and civilian clothes. What happens to you after that is up to you." He walked away to avoid further questions, but glanced back.

Cassius had been about Aris's age when he first met Noble and was taken into the service of the Imperium. Everything he was and everything he knew had come from the Motherworld. After a few years of service, he forgot what it was like to not have every aspect of his life directed by the wishes of the Realm. He turned back to watch the city in flames.

Once inside, Felix shoved Aris toward a bench. He sat down, his body heavy. It seemed like he had been running for days, although it had not been even a few hours. His pounding heart slowed. He felt every trickle of sweat roll from beneath his armpits and down the nape of his neck. The clothing he wore suddenly felt sticky and tight. And nothing would ever be the same again. War warped time as it did minds and souls. Aris sat with his hands clasped on his lap, feeling numb in a vacuum of chaos.

Footfalls and voices brought him back to reality. His eyes, already on the floor, knew whose boots were in front of him. He looked up to see Noble, covered in more blood than when Aris left him. In that moment he *knew*. They were all gone except for him. The last of his father's bloodline. The priests behind Noble chanted and held the staff still coated with his family's blood. There was also that horrible image of a man surrounded by human teeth.

This what he had to show fealty for? Is that what all those innocent people died for? Then, in that moment, he understood why his father met with enemies of the Motherworld. Noble locked eyes with him as he removed his leather gloves and wiped his bloodied face with his bare hands. His vacant eyes shifted as he walked to the other end of the ship, shouting at someone to get him a clean uniform and new boots. Having blood on their hands meant nothing to men like Noble. And men like Cassius kept them there.

Aris stared at the ground, because the priests stood at attention behind their masks and directed themselves at him. He could feel their stares and energy surround him with claustrophobic intention, but he did not know why they stared. It made his cheeks and chest burn with the desire to kill them all, and if he could, he would. Their blood on his hands. *One day*, he thought to himself.

MARA, THE RINGED RED GIANT, DOMINATED THE SKY OF VELDT. THE PLOUGH CAME to an abrupt halt when it hit a large stone beneath the dirt. She dropped to her knees to dig it out. Kora felt the soft, damp soil. She took a handful in her hands and took in its rich aroma. This land, and Mara, gave her a sliver of hope. In death there could be rebirth. The stars told this tale. Here she dared to believe this was true. It also reinforced that there was courage in expanding beyond what one believed to be the only truth. There was courage in accepting death when that expansion was over.

She wondered what it meant for what time she had left, and those who were dead that didn't deserve to be. The ache of her muscles matched the ache of deep sorrow she felt inside. But her body had the ability to recover. Her mind needed to heal, to maybe forget if possible. Here she had found a second chance, even though she didn't believe she deserved one. She rose to her feet again, having moved the stone. The pull of the uraki on the yoke of the plough broke Kora's gaze across the horizon as the day and its labor was nearly done. An *honest* day of work done. The large beast, with a thick bone plate on the front of its face, snorted and kicked its hooves. The fertile soil she tilled stretched in front of her like the darkness of space, the only place she could call home since she was a child.

Except now her feet were firmly planted on the ground. It was a good feeling. Her mind traveled to how many times her life had been overturned, then all the wounds of memory smoothed over so she could live with herself, her past. The soil was cool and damp. She could smell the uraki fertilizer that gave it the scent of tree bark and summer beetles. Honest work amongst honest people. The village lay nestled in a protected valley of immense natural beauty that consisted of homes made from strong forest timber and sod roofs, the longhouse, a stone granary, stables, and the village bell that hung like a silent sentinel. It was simple living, but peaceful.

"Kora!"

Her head turned toward the stone bridge and a familiar voice. Her heart beat a little faster despite the moment of rest. The reddish hue from Mara cast its crimson light against the man who called her name. His tall, lean body was a mere silhouette from where she stood. She still knew who it was: Gunnar. His brown eyes locked onto hers as he approached. Brown hair with blond streaks brushed against his forehead.

He paused and a smile spread across his lips when she looked at him. Before he could get too close, the uraki snorted again and let out a low whine. Gunnar stopped and touched the beast behind its ear to give it a gentle pat. "I thought you were finished. Everyone's up in the longhouse."

Kora glanced toward the longhouse in the distance. People were piling in for a night of celebration. There was still a part of her that held back from completely giving herself to this village. There was always a fear that good things didn't last if you gave yourself to them fully. Being an outsider and remaining that way seemed the safest option. "These are my last rows and I'll be done."

Gunnar searched her face with an expression that said he didn't quite believe her. The atmosphere between them vibrated as densely as the gas giant above them. "All right. Okay. Well, uh, Den was asking where you were. He and his brother got a big snow-elk, a male. He wanted you to see it before he dressed it."

Kora arched one eyebrow. "Why was he asking for me?" She took the reins of the plough to begin her work again.

Gunnar looked confused at this statement. "Well, you know, I thought you two… because he's…"

"You thought," she said over her shoulder. "Move up," she told Gunnar, before calling out to the uraki to move again whilst pulling on the reins. It snorted and huffed past Gunnar, who watched Kora walk toward the horizon. He turned and made his way back to the longhouse now releasing smoke from the lit hearth inside.

As Kora continued her work with her eyes on the soil, she thought if she ended up buried beneath this land many years from now, never leaving, she would get off easy. It wasn't a bad place for a final resting place.

The longhouse sounded like joy and pride. The villagers sat at large rectangular tables eating stout bread with sweet butter, boiled seasonal root vegetables, and drinking ale or last year's summer berry wine that had finished fermenting. The main hearth had a large torso of a beast spinning on a steel spit. Fat dripped from the roasting meat. There was enough for all to enjoy. Their past feasts were on show, with antlers and pelts of all sizes decorating the walls. Some sang out in with slurred words that rose to the high ceilings. Couples sat close and hands crept toward available bare skin. The blush of spring colored their faces.

Three firepits blazed in the center row. The smoky scent of heather wood gave the air a sensual scent. Kora sat eating the last of her meal next to Hagen, the one who had first welcomed her into the village. The man old enough to be her father or grandfather stroked his white beard while pouring her another goblet of wine. What hair he had left was the same shade of silver. His purple lips and teeth showed he had enjoyed his drink that night. "Here is another well-earned tipple."

Kora reached for the goblet and noticed Gunnar looking her way. After finishing her work, she'd changed out of her dusty coveralls and cotton shirt into a pale-yellow dress with a small floral print. Her thin necklace glinted in the firelight. When their eyes locked, his gaze lingered with a stifled longing before turning away. The fire and wine warmed her body. Having eyes on her like that heated something else.

But he never made any advances toward her. It had been too long since she was last touched or kissed so hard it crushed the oxygen out of her body. Before Veldt, her life was about the mission given to her. She had never been in love. Physically satiated, yes. Now she had settled into the calm of one moment at a time and no orders. So many years were dictated by the rigidity of someone else's plans for her.

Hagen noticed the exchange but didn't say anything about it. "How beautiful was that meat tonight? We are truly lucky for our abundance."

Kora took a sip of the wine. "It's been a while since we've had fresh meat. Forgot how good it is."

Hagen nodded and drank his wine. "Oh, Den said they saw the summer herds returning. Maybe three days' ride away. He was asking for you."

A smile crept over Kora's lips. Den was a different story to Gunnar. He was a natural hunter with just enough aggression to get what he wanted without being overly mean or domineering. "I heard. And, yes, it's quite impressive."

Hagen leaned into the table to catch Kora's gaze. "Which one? The animal? Or the hunter?"

Kora cocked her head to the side and shook it. She turned from Hagen and searched the crowd until she saw

Den. Her eyes traveled the length of his body when he wasn't looking. That man was all muscle, hair, and probably cock. He didn't incite love, far from it. But something very primal stirred within. Nocturnal animals instinctually know when to come out at night. Den glanced her way, feeling the weight of her stare.

The moment was broken by the loud blast of the Veldt ceremonial horn by Sven the carpenter's apprentice. The village leader, Sindri, stood tall at the stand. The room fell silent as he cleared his throat and gave his beard, with three braids decorated with silver cuffs, a stroke, wiping ale foam from his top lip. His blue eyes beamed with pride as he looked at the villagers. The night's alcohol had given his skin a pink glow and his bald head shined from his seat in the firelight.

"My people, my friends, it is my honor to stand before you with winter bested and spring now in full bloom. The fields tilled and nearly seeded. It is my duty as the head of this table, nay, community to remind you that the gods of the harvest demand a tribute."

Sindri took his goblet from his table and turned toward his wife next to him. Her face glowed with love and devotion, her cheeks rosy from the heat of the room and wine.

"An offering. But we all know it is the thrusting of hips and the loud sounds of pleasure that summon the seedlings to sprout. So fuck hard tonight. Fuck for the harvest. Fuck for the very food we eat. Fuck for the gods!"

A chorus of cheers and affirmations rang out. Sindri

raised his glass to his flustered red face as his wife pulled on the leather strap and bronze buckle at his waist. He dipped down and kissed her with wine trailing on his beard.

"Easy, woman. Let me finish my civic duty. Then I'll finish my duty as a husband. Wait… did I say to fuck?"

The room erupted into cheers and laughter after he said this.

"Let's have some music!" Sindri called out. "Some music to get us in the mood."

Kora's eyes darted toward Gunnar, who looked at her too. However, he immediately looked away. He was by far the most sober in the room. In her periphery she could see Den staring in her direction. She turned her head to see him gulping his beer with his eyes still fixed on her. He licked his lips and smiled. Her eyes trailed from his mouth to the half-open cotton shirt revealing part of his chest and a tuft of hair. She imagined his body sculpted from hard work handling animals in the wilderness of Veldt. Her thoughts went wild. She raised her goblet to him. Den hit his brother in the chest with his empty horn of ale and began to approach her.

Hagen whispered in her ear. "I will make myself scarce now. Too much wine for this old man. I will see you later." He rose to his feet, leaving her on her own with Den.

In the distance, she could see Gunnar looking in their direction. He finished his conversation with one of the villagers and turned to walk out of the longhouse without looking back.

Den slid next to her, where Hagen had sat moments before. "You need a little company the rest of the night? It's far too early to go to bed."

She smiled and looked into his eyes. "Is it?"

He leaned against the table and closer to her. She could smell his sweat and the lingering scent of soap on his skin. "How about I leave first, and when you find yourself wandering through the village, you stop in front of my door?"

She gave him a half smile and leaned toward his ear, whispering something that embarrassed and excited him in equal measure.

Den rose to his feet and glanced around the room. The remaining villagers pretended not to watch them. He left, walking briskly without saying goodbye to anyone. Kora grabbed her goblet and knocked back the last of her wine. It tasted sweet on her tongue and warm as it ran down her throat. She walked out of the longhouse, not paying attention to any eyes that might be watching her leaving right after Den.

Den would get exactly what he wanted that night, and so would she. Her heart quickened with each step closer to his house. The anticipation of exploring a new body sent waves of excitement throughout her body. When she arrived at his door, she ran her fingers through her hair then knocked once.

He opened the door shirtless. His home was dark except for two candles burning in the middle of a table. "You showed up."

"Wasn't ready to go home."

He stepped aside from the doorway to let her in. Except for Hagen, this was the first time she had been in a man's home alone since she arrived. The walls were filled with mounted hunting trophies, antlers of all sizes, feathers, claws and teeth, but besides that there was little in the way of decoration. He kept his home clean and orderly, which was not out of step with his personality in the village. In the back she could see the closed door to what she assumed was his bedroom. Her eyes shifted back to Den, who stood looking at her with the same intensity she imagined he had when hunting these animals. He could pin her to the wall that night, or the floor, as long as he didn't stop until she was satisfied.

Kora walked closer to him. The flickering candlelight accentuated his muscles. She touched his chest while looking up at his face. Her fingertips trailed to the waist of his trousers. She could feel his growing arousal. Without saying a word or giving her any warning, he lifted her with both hands on either side of her waist. She held onto his neck while her strong, thick thighs wrapped around his waist. He held her with one arm under her ass as he walked toward the bedroom and burst through the door. One foot kicked the door closed behind him before dropping her onto the bed after three big strides.

He tried to kiss her on the lips, but she twisted her face so his lips would land on her neck. When he tried again without success, he moved lower. One by one, he unbuttoned her dress. His mouth moved to her breasts and nipples. Small nibbles kept them erect and caused soft moans to escape her mouth. This made him try to move lower, but that wasn't what she came for. She wanted what she felt earlier, she wanted to be fucked by Den, not for him to make love to her. She looked to the ceiling in agitation as he tried to go down on her. She grabbed him by the arms to pull him up. He did as instructed.

She watched Den take off his trousers as she pulled off her panties. The tip of his wet, hard cock, the shape of a scythe, glinted beneath the light of the two full moons. His thighs were solid tree trunks that rippled with muscle. All his weight could crush her. She just wanted him to work on her like he would to tame a Veldt stallion. Steady, firm, knowing when to wait and when to ride hard. He was everything she needed for the night. Sometimes the aching need to be taken care of won, if only for a few hours, if only physical.

Loneliness was part of Kora's shadow. Nights like those were flaming arrows in the dark, a signal she was still alive. Unbridled ecstasy without strings attached had the power to soothe the restless soul. And she was a restless soul. Den was fresh meat to satisfy the hunger inside of her. The desire inside of her, only rhythmic thrusts bringing her to a full orgasm would do.

Without words she rolled on top of him. Kora straddled him and pulled off her dress. A large puckered scar ran from her shoulder, down her back, and ended on her thigh. His large hands held her hips and round ass tight, as if he were taking control of a two-uraki plough caught in wet, deep soil. She grinded on his eager cock without looking at his face with her head thrown back.

Her brown skin began to bead with sweat the faster she moved her body to squeeze the most amount of pleasure from that moment. The pinch in her lower back from grinding only accentuated the pleasure. The excitement leaking from between her legs lubricated her thighs. She bit her lip and cried out as he pulled on her hips faster. She brought one hand between her legs to create more tension. Tender, engorged flesh tightened for a hard release. The harder he thrust upwards, the faster she moved her fingers until her entire body warmed with the tension of ecstasy cracking open and oozing with the same richness of egg yolk. His heavy breathing matched hers as he orgasmed shortly after with a loud grunt.

She fell onto his chest before moving next to him. He lay there with ragged breath and eyes closed. It wasn't long before he was asleep. She wondered what it would be like to lie next to the same person year after year under the same roof. The idea was a foreign concept, unreachable as unmapped star systems since she had sat in her first dropship headed for battle. That is not what brought her to his bed. His wide chest rose and fell with the heaviness of falling into a deep sleep. She wondered about Gunnar. Did he sleep alone? The village was so small, she would know if he didn't. She sat up and quietly gathered her clothing and dressed in the waning candlelight. She blew them out before leaving. Without looking back, she left Den's home.

Kora wandered in the dark toward the river. The moons crowned the rolling hills and tree line. God, she loved the quiet beauty in this place. Post-orgasm, her body felt lax and content. The sweat between her breasts and shoulder blades dried with the breeze cooling her down. The sound of the river in constant motion relaxed her. She enjoyed sharing a home with Hagen, who hadn't demanded anything of her since arriving. Before entering the house, she grabbed a rag from the clothesline and dipped into a bucket of cool, clean water. She wiped the remaining sweat and the lingering scent of Den off her skin. As quietly as she could, she crept inside, trying not to wake Hagen. He was still awake and reading in bed by lamplight. He looked to Kora as she moved toward her bed. She sat down and removed her boots.

"Den is a good man," Hagen said.

"You should be asleep," Kora said.

"He's the best hunter among us. And a loyal friend. Have you thought of a more permanent relationship? I know that he's amenable to the idea. He's asked me himself."

Kora looked at Hagen. "It's easy between us. Does it have to be more than that?"

His aging eyes had a softness to them. There was always honesty reflected back. "It's just, uh… That would be your last step to becoming a full member of this community. I'm telling you, this is home now."

Kora knew Hagen meant well. There wasn't a nasty bone in his body. "I want that to be true."

Hagen continued to look at her with almost pleading eyes. "Kora, having a child and marrying would give you the stability I think you want. And it would be here."

Kora sat at the edge of her bed with her nightshirt next to her. She lifted it to her nose. It had the faint scent of black blossom and the breeze of a warm spring day. Hagen had provided for her generously from the first day he brought her back here and nursed back to life more than her broken body. He had helped her soul.

"You know, the two seasons I've spent here have given me happiness… that I don't deserve. But understand, I am a child of war. To truly love and be loved, I… I don't know if I'm capable of either."

"Don't say that. The village has warmed to you, trusts you. You must feel that. This can be and is your home. My Liv would have been about your age now and her mother would have loved you like a daughter. I am so happy you could use what she left behind. I didn't have the heart to throw any of it out."

Kora stood to close the fabric partition between their beds and change for the evening. "The very idea of love, of family, was beaten out of me. I was taught that love is weakness. And I… I don't know how that will ever change."

"You're wrong," Hagen said. "I've watched you change. You're not the same person you were when you came here. They say people don't change. It's nonsense. That's all they do. Constantly. I hope you can see that one day."

Kora lifted her gaze to meet Hagen's kind countenance. Hagen gave her a loving but stern stare. "War happened to you. You are not war, but you must conquer your fears like a warrior." He had a fist lifted to his chest as he said this. Kora softened and gave him the kind of smile a daughter would give a father. He was all heart and his tone reflected this. "Thank you. Go to sleep. Sorry to have disturbed you."

He continued to look at her. "Just promise me you will think about it."

Kora nodded. "You should get some rest."

"Yeah." Hagen leaned over the small table and turned off the lamp. Kora pulled closed the black curtains.

As she lay in bed, she hoped Den wouldn't think her cruel for leaving him if he did want a relationship deeper than great sex. And a child? Unless she divulged the entire truth of her past, he would never understand the depth of her wounds. What kind of life would it be for a family to live in the shadow of a wanted outlaw of a woman? Her heart remained in pieces too broken to hold the type of love a child required.

KORA ROSE EARLY TO JOIN THE VILLAGE BUSTLING IN THE EARLY LIGHT OF dawn, leaving Hagen to sleep. He would join later because it was seeding day. She began in the large stone granary with Sam, the young woman who was not yet spoken for in the village, but it wouldn't be long since she was close to turning eighteen. She was bright and pretty with straw-colored hair and cornflower-blue eyes. But beyond her appearance, she had a good heart and a light, playful soul that still possessed the innocence of a young girl.

Gunnar stood near one of the granary doors, taking inventory of the sacks of seeds and dividing them amongst the villagers for seeding. He kept thorough records for the village so there would always be enough. As Kora opened her apron for seeds, Gunnar looked in her eyes. Both paused. She gave him a smile before making her way into the field. She wondered if he had any inkling of her night with Den, but Den was the one who hadn't been afraid to make his move.

She felt a pang of sadness looking at Gunnar. The village was too small to have them both. And that urge was very much there. On Veldt, she could live the life denied to her by Balisarius and her career in the Imperium military. Sam followed behind her. There were already dozens of villagers dusting the dewy tilled fields with seeds. Kora began to do the same and Sam joined her. She slightly elbowed Kora and gave her a sly smile. "I noticed you left early last night. Were you tired?"

Kora didn't look up from grabbing a handful of seeds. She tried to prevent herself from matching Sam's smile, but didn't do a good enough job concealing a smirk. "That's right. I thought I'd make it an early night."

Sam stood upright and placed one hand on her hip with a teasing look. "I thought you were doing your part for the harvest, because as I walked home, I passed Den's house, and that's truly what it sounded like. Your cries alone will sprout these seeds."

Kora kept her face neutral but still didn't make eye contact with Sam. "Sam, I don't know what you're talking about."

"I think you do?" Sam said innocently.

"What about you, Sam?"

The young girl shook her head. "I don't think my person will be found in this village. I'd like someone totally different from me but who could also understand what it's like to not have family the way most people do." Sam paused then crossed her arms. "He might fall from the sky for all I know."

Kora shook her head and chuckled. "You sure you want another stranger like me?" She playfully flicked the few seeds in her hands to Sam, who was about to do the same until her eyes traveled from Kora to the sky. Lips parted in silent awe. Kora's smile dropped with Sam's change in demeanor. She looked over her shoulder to see what had caught Sam's attention. What she saw made her drop her apron, spilling her seeds onto her boots and the ground.

Over the fertile hills and just beyond the horizon, a colossal warship entered the atmosphere. Instant recognition and terror held Kora in its tight grip. A thousand thoughts with the weight of a herd of uraki stampeded her mind. Kora scanned the field in panic as the rest of the villagers stared in curious awe at the ship. None of them could fathom what hell had entered their world.

"No," Kora whispered, before turning to run toward the village. The beat of her racing heart thumped in her eardrums as her arms pumped hard. Fallen hair whipped against her eyes and open mouth. The longhouse was just in sight, and next to it the massive six-foot village bell that hung solemnly in the shape of a cannon, hanging from the stump of a tree cut from the original site of the village and placed into stone. It had been there since anyone living could remember. Runes and village scenes decorated the surface of the bell. Her feet hit the stone bridge with loud slaps as she crossed the river that divided the village and the fields.

Kora wrenched the heavy hammer from its wooden hold. Her muscles flexed as she groaned through gritted teeth. One hard swing after another made her ears ring from the reverberation of the gong. She pummeled the bell until Sindri shuffled out of the longhouse, bleary-eyed from the night before. Kora dropped the hammer to the ground and pointed a weary finger toward the sky. Sindri's gaze followed her direction. He took a step back with mouth agape. "What do you think they want?"

Sweat poured from Kora's scalp. It was better than tears because *they* didn't respond to tears or pain. She shook her head as she caught her breath. "Everything."

Looking like a lost child, Sindri no longer possessed his bravado from the night before. His position as leader was not something he fought for or proved himself worthy of. His uncle held the position and made Sindri his successor. Armed conflict was not something this village had experienced. With little to complain about, the village accepted this. "What should we do?"

"Gather all the elders and adults. Stay together."

Sindri nodded and rushed toward the fields. Kora's eyes returned to the ship. It had a name: a dreadnought. A familiar hate bubbled in the pit of her belly like too much ale all at once. Her exhaustion turned to malice. The universe was supposedly infinite, but *they* made it feel entirely too small with too many corners to be backed into. It didn't matter if they came for her or for some other reason. You did not want one of those ships in your orbit or landing on your world. She didn't know what they could possibly want with this village, or these people who didn't possess anything for battle.

The din of the longhouse had returned to the volume of the previous night. However, it was not revelry. It was worry, and question after question from the villagers. Kora stood in the back with arms crossed, observing in silence. Sindri and Gunnar stood at the front, attempting to listen to five conversations at once while staring each other down. Red-faced Sindri paced in a circle with his hands clasped behind his back.

"Gunnar, I don't care what the potential upside might be, a warship hanging over our land cannot be good."

Gunnar didn't hide his frustration as he moved to catch Sindri's roving, twitching eyes.

"That's your problem. Your first reaction is always fear."

Greta, the uraki breeder, cleared her throat and spoke above the cacophony of voices. "Assuming they come down to talk, we could at least hear them out to see what their intentions are."

A murmur of villagers speaking to each other rose after Greta spoke.

Gunnar took this opportunity to further his point. He turned toward the crowd. "Exactly! The Motherworld has deep pockets. I'm simply saying maybe we can get a better price from our friends in low orbit there rather than having to deal with the cutthroats in Providence, selling our grain to God only knows."

Most of those in the crowd whispered in agreement. Sindri's eyes narrowed, ignoring the room. "Don't act like we don't know you've been selling our surplus grain to the enemies of that ship up there. I wonder what they would say if they found out where our excess went last year."

Gunnar stood his ground, expressionless. "Well, I'm no revolutionary. They offered the best price. I don't care about their cause."

Sindri did not capitulate. "Obviously."

Gunnar scanned the eager eyes and ears of the fellow villagers he had known his entire life. His eyes softened for a moment. "Sindri, I don't have a side, only this community. That's my only loyalty. And I say we start by showing them goodwill, not fear. That we are their partners, not their adversaries, right?"

Kora remained tight-lipped with her arms crossed throughout the entire debate. But this had gone far enough. She couldn't blame them. None of them knew what threat loomed above their heads like a thunderstorm ready to release destruction. She pushed past bodies to the front. Den caught her eye; he gave her a nod but didn't stop her.

"Did you say 'partner', Gunnar?"

"I di— I did. Is that a problem?" he asked.

Kora stood between Sindri and Gunnar, facing the villagers. "That ship does not represent prosperity. Its purpose is to destroy, to subjugate, to enslave. Partnership is not in its vocabulary. Give them what they ask for. But volunteer nothing about how fertile this land is. And hope they leave before digging too deep into who Gunnar sold last year's grain to."

"Right," Gunnar said, deflated by Kora's words, as if it was a personal attack. The rest of the room went silent. Gunnar scrambled as Sindri's face turned to stone. "If I may, Sindri…"

"I've heard enough. We will volunteer nothing. Is that clear?" snapped the village leader.

Kora looked at Gunnar again. She opened her mouth to speak when one of the children, a boy of ten named Eljun, ran through the door. He panted with rosy cheeks. "They're coming! They're coming! They're coming!"

Kora, Sindri, and Gunnar all exchanged glances before striding toward the door. Kora paused in front of Eljun, who looked up to her with round, innocent eyes. She reached out to touch his cheek and pulled her hand away again. "Hide. Don't come out until your parents' voices call you, even if it seems safe." He nodded and ran off. The sound of the dropships could be heard in the distance. She walked past Eljun and into the village.

The harsh reflection of sunlight and Mara bouncing off the three dropships blinded the villagers. Kora didn't need to see what would occur next. She knew. They landed in the center of the freshly seeded field. Soil and seed flew in all directions. There was a moment of pause before the doors opened and long ramps extended across the dirt.

A man in impeccable dress, an officer's cap worn low, and shiny boots devoid of scuff or dirt led the way with another in a similar, but less ornate, uniform. Six others who must have been some sort of religious sect shuffled behind in long robes, their faces masked. The rest piling from the dropships were soldiers in light Imperium armor and dirty striped trousers, carrying the type of weapons the villagers did not possess. There was never any need.

Sindri and Gunnar stepped across the bridge to meet the leader halfway. Sindri mustered all his charismatic charm. "Hello. I am Sindri, father of this village. Welcome."

The man from the drop ship brought one hand over his heart. "I'm Admiral Atticus Noble. Loyal representative of the slain king. I welcome you to his warm embrace." He looked across the vast fields and village. "Please, Father, tell me about this beautiful village."

Noble wrapped his arms around Sindri with the muscular grip of a spotted bog serpent. Sindri hesitated before returning the hug, but less tight. Immediately behind Noble stood a man who had to be a lower-ranking officer. He wasn't a priest or a regular soldier. He could have been a statue with his obedient stillness and silence. Further back, Sindri could see the soldiers giving the village a cold stare, with weapons in hand and fingers near triggers. Noble broke from Sindri, yet still gripped his shoulders with his fingertips digging into his flesh. He gave Sindri a large grin that seemed too friendly for just meeting. "As you are the father of this beautiful village, please tell me all about it. I want to know *everything*."

Sindri glanced back at Kora, then to Noble.

"Walk with me up to our longhouse. We can have a cup of ale and I will tell you about life here."

Noble removed his hands from Sindri and gave him a short nod. "Oh. Sounds perfect. Lead the way. It has been some time since I have had a good, rustic ale. Cassius will also join us, and the others shall follow." He twisted enough to extend his hand toward Cassius, who said nothing but observed everything.

Sindri turned to face the silent villagers, watching the entire encounter. They made way for Sindri and Noble to walk toward the longhouse. Cassius, the statue of a man, walked close behind. Close enough to hear anything that was said. His eyes captured everything. Kora followed as closely as possible in the crowd to hear the conversation. Noble caught her gaze for a moment before looking away. Small squares of fabric attached to strings zigzagged across the village blew in the breeze above their heads as they walked.

"We've carved out a simple life here. And we take pride in the love of our community, and the hard work it takes to survive here," said Sindri in a calm, even tone.

Noble intently inspected the villagers and the buildings. His eyes caught three healthy uraki tied to a corral not far from the longhouse. They nuzzled into a trough of food and water.

"Well, your people seem healthy and well fed. As their leader, much of that prosperity must be credited to you."

Sindri shook his head. "No, we are a community. The credit is no one person's."

"Oh, I know that in the best of times the credit's

shared. But when the stores are empty, you know where the responsibility falls."

Sindri stopped and faced Noble at the entrance of the longhouse. "The weight of the leader, I suppose."

Noble clapped his leather-gloved hands and pursed his lips. "So you... you understand the feeling of, of, like a father, the need to feed your children, yeah? I was hoping that your land and the people of Veldt might be able to help as we search for a small band of revolutionaries hiding in this very system. Who my commander, the Regent Balisarius, bid me find and bring to justice."

"We are humble farmers, far removed from the politics of the Motherworld."

"And still you can serve."

Sindri glanced toward the crowd with Kora and Gunnar near the front, not knowing what to say. Noble studied him with the eyes of a predator. He placed a hand on Sindri's shoulder and squeezed.

"Hmm. The rebels we seek have been attacking our supply ports. Led by a woman named Devra Bloodaxe, and her brother Darrian. Their capture is inevitable. However, it's taken longer than anticipated, and we found ourselves admittedly low on stores. And as you know or may have heard, an army runs on its stomach. I was thinking of a partnership, where you supply us with food. Whatever you have to spare, of course. In exchange, you're compensated at... Let's call it triple the market value, shall we? With that windfall, you'll be able to buy plenty of harvesters, robots, and won't have to do this difficult work by hand."

"We believe that doing the work by hand connects us to the land and honors these sacred fields that give us life," said Sindri, trying to not to seem too eager or aloof. However, his lips trying to smile appeared strained.

Noble removed his hand and extended his palm toward the villagers. "Well, there's always the peace of mind knowing that you're playing an invaluable role in the important mission of rooting out enemies of the Motherworld."

Sindri narrowed his eyes and quickly glanced into the crowd. Kora's chin was close to her chest and her arms were folded. She discreetly shook her head. The Realm had a cunning way to make their victims believe everything would be fine.

"It's quite a proposal."

"Yes."

"If only we had some surplus to offer. You see, the land is rocky and yields barely enough to feed ourselves. So, it is with sincere apologies that we must decline the offer. However, we are grateful for the presence of such a benevolent and powerful protector."

Noble paused, looking around. Vast fields that teased fertility were in every direction. What could have been a glower disappeared from his face in an instant. Noble tilted his head and gave Sindri a soft smile. "Huh. No surplus? None at all? Huh. But your land looks so fertile. Your fields seem larger than what your population might need."

"Of course, I understand how it might seem. Yet the

scale of the planting is evidence of the poor soil. And our harsh winters only add to the short season. Now, what do you say we share that cup of ale, eh?"

Noble looked at the villagers one by one. "Sorry. It's just... I mean, look at these beautiful people. I can't imagine these glowing complexions are nourished by barren fields, that's all. Now... who's the man or woman among you who oversees the harvest? There must be one of you whose thumb is greener than the rest. Someone?"

No one said anything, but a few eyes gravitated toward Gunnar. Noble's eyes soon followed. He pointed at him as if his finger had the power to pin him to the wall. "Hmmm?"

Gunnar watched the crowd look toward him and move away at the same time. He lifted his face slightly and stared directly at Noble. "Yes, sir. That is me."

"Good."

"Yes, I... I oversee the harvest."

Noble motioned for him to come closer. "Oh, well, if these people trust you, then so do I. Just trying to understand how I could be so wrong about what this land could yield, that's all."

Gunnar couldn't look in Sindri's direction. "Well, sir. Sindri, our beloved father, is always looking out for the welfare of our village, and so insists on keeping reserves in case of famine or drought, which as you know, is the responsibility of a leader. But, but we have been lucky th—these last few seasons and our surplus has been more than we can store. So, there might be... a chance that we can spare a small amount. Depending, of course, on the scale of your needs."

Noble's lips curled to a half smile, followed by his eyes turning toward Sindri. "Mm, good, good. Yeah, I mean, it's always wise to hold some in reserve, isn't it, Father? Yet, I am confused. Curious as to why you should have me believe this land could barely yield enough to feed your people. Seems that wasn't entirely true."

Gunnar stammered and stepped closer to Noble. His hands waved in the air with panic. "No, no, no, wait, wait. Admiral, uh, no one is trying to mislead you. Sindri simply has a slightly more conservative view on reserves than I do. But we're both excited about a possible partnership. Just bear in mind the reality of what we can supply."

Noble twisted his head toward Sindri. "Father, who is this exactly?"

Gunnar attempted to stammer a response. "Uh, my—"

Sindri's cheeks flushed, his voice turned gruff. "He's of no consequence. I have been empowered by my people to speak for them. This man has no authority here. You would be wise to ignore him."

Noble looked out to the crowd. The tension from the scene stifled any movement or sound from the villagers present. "Well… a rift. It's not quite the idyllic community I'd first seen."

Kora cursed under her breath and moved closer to the three men. Sindri's wife walked to one of the tables where the ale and goblets were stored. She poured a single cup to offer Noble.

"Father, if I may offer you some advice when dealing with subordinates who need to be kept in place. I find people can lose sight of the stakes and sometimes need a gentle reminder of just how those with power deal with those without."

Kora's eyes shifted as the priests moved in unison toward Noble. Cassius stared on without a twitch or ounce of emotion. He only distanced himself from the priests as they passed, as if they were repellent to him. One of the priests held an oversized femur plated in embossed bronze. She quickly looked toward Gunnar with worry in her eyes. When the priest holding the staff stood next to Noble, he extended it toward him. Noble smiled as he took it into his hands. "Let me show you what I mean."

Sindri's gaze followed Noble until the staff swung above his head. Noble brought it down directly into the middle of his forehead, splitting it open as Sindri fell into the crowd. Blood splattered across those directly in front of him. There was a collective gasp, but no one moved as Noble continued to pummel Sindri's open skull. Noble's face twisted and he let out sharp breaths as he used all his strength during the attack. Sindri's wife rushed through the crowd, screaming his name. A large crack previously unheard in the village stopped her lamentations. Without hesitation, one of the Krypteian Guards behind the priests sliced her across the back with his sword made from oracle steel. The blue heat killed her in an instant. Her body fell next to Sindri. Their blood co-mingled and pooled on the floor.

Noble looked toward the villagers. "Anyone else?" His dead eyes suggested he had no preference. Ending every bloodline there was as reasonable as sparing the villagers, just slightly more tiresome. The room remained silent. Noble pointed the bloody staff toward Gunnar. "You."

Gunnar stared at the bodies of Sindri and his wife with his lips parted. Slowly he looked up. "What did you do?"

"When can I expect my harvest?" asked Noble.

"Oh, I—I don't—" Gunnar stammered.

Noble took a step closer to Gunnar and placed the staff beneath his chin, leaving a bloody print on his rough cotton tunic. "I said, tell me, *partner*, when I can expect my harvest."

Gunnar glanced at Kora, who stood with every muscle as tight as bowstrings. His eyes sunk. "Uh, uh, nine, nine weeks."

Noble removed the staff from Gunnar's body and nodded. He gave him a chipper smile as if there were no dead bodies in the room, no blood on his staff, no skull fragments on his boots. "Very well. In ten weeks, I will return. You will have ten thousand bushels prepared for my ship. I know that the outlaws I seek were on this world last season and that someone sold them a few thousand bushels. I hope your lies died with your father."

The villagers began to whisper amongst themselves. Noble ignored them as he wiped blood from his uniform and handed the staff back to the priest, who accepted it with a deep bow. In a voice loud enough for all to hear, Noble faced the crowd. "Also, I will be leaving men and weapons here to ensure your side of the arrangement is upheld. Be gracious to them."

Now fully engaged, Gunnar spoke up. "Twelve—Uh, we barely produce twelve thousand bushels. We—We'll starve to death. I—I don't understand what you want."

Expressionless, Noble stepped closer to Gunnar and locked eyes. "Well, it's simple. I want everything."

Noble walked past Gunnar without looking at the villagers. Cassius gave Gunnar a stern glare before following the priests and Noble back to the dropships. The priests began to follow, with their voices beginning to hum until loud foreign chants filled the longhouse. One stopped and extracted a single tooth from Sindri's mouth with metal pliers. He placed the tooth in the mosaic of teeth surrounding the portrait of Princess Issa.

When they were gone, wails rose to the rafters. Some fell to their knees, others moved to see to their dead leader and his wife. Gunnar and Kora were the only ones who remained still as they stared at each other. She moved to walk toward him with pity in her eyes, but he shook his head and raised his hand. Kora would never pour salt in his wound with an "I told you so," but she knew he needed a little time, even though it was time they couldn't spare. He walked out of the longhouse alone.

Dirt spun into the atmosphere in mini tornadoes as the dropships left for *The King's Gaze*. Left behind were Imperium soldiers and large metal crates with what they needed to camp until Noble's return in ten weeks.

Faunus, the most senior soldier, in his fifties with thick

black hair cut in the traditional Imperium style for all soldiers, short and cut horizontally across the forehead, assessed his surroundings. His eyes landed on the granary. "All right, listen up. I need all of this gear moved to this big stone building. That should suit us for now. Marcus, you're gonna help me evict the current residents from our new home. Copy?" He pointed toward the stone building.

"Copy you, boss. Copy you," Marcus said.

The rest of the men begin to follow his orders, with one of the youngest hesitating. Faunus's eyes narrowed. "That goes for you too, Aris. No special treatment."

Aris jumped to move while Faunus approached one of the men, about ten years younger than himself, blond and blue-eyed. "Come on, Marcus." Both men left to inspect the granary.

Aris walked to the last of the crates, the largest left behind. He looked at it in curiosity. There was ancient writing etched into a panel next to a lever. He glanced around before wrapping his fingers around it and pulling it down. Mechanical whirring and clicks could be heard from inside. Aris took a few steps back as the middle of the metal crate opened like a yawning mouth. From inside a figure stood. Aris's eyes went wide with the excitement a child would express. "Battle robot," he whispered to himself.

The robot had no facial features except for fourteen small circles on its faceplate. Two of them for eyes glowed like quasars. It only had the basic anatomy of a human, constructed from its armor that matched the color of the soldiers' armor and uniform. The script on the panel in the style of the old kingdom also decorated the robot's metal form. In the center of its chest was an image of a simple chalice in a circle. Its head turned toward Aris. An even-toned voice spoke. "I am JC1435 of the Mechanics Militarium, defender of the king. Correction, of the slain king. It is my honor to serve."

Aris looked at the robot with boyish wonder. "I'm Private Aris. We're moving these supplies over to that building, if you wouldn't mind lending a hand."

"Thank you, Private Aris. That falls perfectly into my protocols."

The robot stepped from the crate and began to work. He made Aris feel a little less alone. A robot was far better company than the soldiers he had been with for the last six months after he completed his training.

Marcus and Faunus stood against the wall of the stone bridge, watching the villagers in the fields and their men set up camp around the granary. Faunus packed a bone pipe with ground hempil leaves when Sam approached them with a jug of cold water. Both men's gazes slithered the entire length of her body. Before she could speak, Marcus snatched the jug from her hands and drank with greed. Water dribbled down his face and onto his shirt. His eyes stopped on Sam, who stood watching him. "Now, what in the name of the old gods are you looking at?" he sneered with malice.

Sam's eyes shined bright with innocence and sunlight

despite their rudeness. "I'm sorry, I was just waiting to see if you needed some more water."

"Some more water?" Marcus grunted and spat on the ground next to Sam. She hurried away before he could say any more.

Faunus watched her rush off while elbowing Marcus. "That's how I like them. Young, strong enough to put up a fight. I like some blood in my mouth when I fuck."

Marcus chuckled before he stopped and took a step forward. He pointed to the field. "Boss. Look." He howled and beat his chest with one fist. "They left us a Jimmy. It's a Jimmy, man. I didn't know we had any of those left."

Faunus scrunched his face as he strained to look. "For fuck's sake…"

Marcus seemed marveled by the sight. "You know they won't fight anymore, boss."

Faunus watched the robot with suspicion and puffed on his pipe. "What do you mean, they won't fight anymore?"

Marcus gave him a malicious grin and lifted his rifle. "It's something in their programming. Once the king was killed, they just laid down their weapons and refused to fight. Just watch, no matter what I do, he doesn't fight back." The two men began to walk toward Jimmy.

In the distance, Aris worked beside Jimmy, moving crates. He carefully stacked a few on top of the load in Jimmy's arms. "Right, careful. The ground's uneven till you get to the bridge."

"Thank you, Private Aris, but I believe I can manage," Jimmy said.

A loud boom rang out across the patch of land. The uraki bellowed and stomped in reaction to the sudden noise. Boxes flew into the air and Jimmy fell to the ground. Both Marcus and Faunus laughed and moved closer to Jimmy. Marcus kept Jimmy in his crosshairs.

"Hey! Careful with that stuff, you stupid machine. I'll turn you into scrap, you dumbshit. You hear me? You're not hearing me." With the robot still on the ground, both soldiers hovered over him. Marcus sent another bullet into Jimmy at close range, causing the robot to jerk awkwardly into a pile of uraki dung. Marcus howled in wicked laughter. The uraki bellowed again and stomped off.

Aris jumped in front of a seated Jimmy. "Hey! Stop!"

Marcus raised his rifle and pointed it at Aris. "What if I shoot you instead, huh?"

Aris remained still as he protected Jimmy. The villagers stopped their work and watched the stand-off. Marcus placed his finger on the trigger as he approached Aris. "I could kill you right now and no one would care. Would they?"

"Then why would I move?" said Aris with enough sorrow-filled strength and defiance to make Marcus clench his jaw and tap his index finger on the trigger as he pressed his weapon beneath Aris's chin.

"That's enough," shouted Faunus.

"What do you say? Wanna die?" Marcus said, gun still trained on Aris.

"C'mon, boy," Aris replied.

"I said, enough," Faunus said, not used to having to

repeat himself. Marcus shot him an annoyed glance before lowering his weapon. A collective breath was released by the villagers and Aris. He looked away from Marcus to see Sam watching. Their eyes met. "Get these crates into that house now, Private," Faunus said.

Jimmy's metallic joints let out a creak. Faunus looked down at him, inspecting the damage. "Are you malfunctioning?"

Jimmy began to rise to his feet. "No, sir."

"Get up. Go to the river. Clean yourself." Faunus looked across the soldiers and villagers gawking. "The rest of you, stop staring. Get back to work."

Jimmy touched the plate that would be his face then looked at his hands. His neck twisted as he registered the smeared dung on his fingers. He nodded and walked off.

"Get back to work, you assholes," said Marcus, waving his rifle toward everyone.

Faunus snatched the weapon out of Marcus's hand. "You too, Marcus!"

Aris grabbed a small crate and shoved it into Marcus's hands. Marcus had no choice but to obey the order to work.

Jimmy wandered to the river and walked along the banks, away from the soldiers and village. He inspected the uraki and Veldt horses that wandered in a pasture. When he lifted his hands toward them, they allowed him to touch them and come close. He continued on until he reached a part of the river that opened to the full vista of the mountains. He took slow steps into the smooth-running water that appeared crystal clear and clean. Small fish swam past his ankle joints. He wanted to exist here, be as free as those fish swimming past and the small insects hovering above the water, or buzzing around the blanket of wildflowers on the bank that gave the air a sweet scent.

Water dripped from Jimmy's body as he sat at the edge of the river. The sun bled across the mountains as it set over Veldt. The hue was heightened by the red giant always looming overhead.

"Excuse me." A small voice made Jimmy turn away from the peaceful sight before him. Sam stood with a towel in hand, offering it to the stranger.

With a gentle touch, Jimmy took the towel from her hand. "Thank you. That is kind." He wiped the water from his hands and face.

She remained with feet firmly planted, studying him from head to toe. "You're a soldier?"

Jimmy nodded. "Long ago."

Sam fiddled with the hem of the apron over her dress and then made to sit down. "Do you mind? I'm Sam."

Jimmy upturned a palm beside him. "Please."

Sam bounded to the rock and gave him a wide smile. His featureless face tilted to one side. The light from his small eye sockets glowed brighter.

Her silky honey-colored hair glistened like spun gold in the warm light. Bright orange-red from the kissing sun and red giant reflected off the water and twinkled in her eyes.

"Tell me, Sam. Do you know the story of our slain king and his beautiful daughter, the Princess Issa?"

Sam shook her head. Strands of hair fell to frame her youthful face as she plucked yellow and white wildflowers surrounding the bank. "I don't." Sam continued to fiddle with the flowers as Jimmy began to speak.

"Well, you remind me of her. In myth, she was called the Chalice or the Redeemer. She was *pueri salvatoris*. And even before she was born, I and my brothers pledged everything we were, everything that dwells inside this metal skin, to fight in her name. So, when word reached us on some distant battlefield that she, as prophesied, had been born of flesh and blood into our world, I felt a great warmth for the universe and trusted that this child would stop the madness of war that had so clouded the minds of the men who commanded us.

"As she grew, stories reached me that she was indeed the one foretold—for it was said she had the power to heal and more, that she possessed limitless kindness and wisdom beyond her years. She was to usher in a new age of peace and compassion. And bring us home."

Sam reached out and traced the chalice on Jimmy's chest with her index fingertip. "She was magic."

Jimmy looked to the river again. "She was more than magic. You see, a king is a man, and a man can fail or betray. But a myth is indestructible. Or so they thought. Because on the day of her coronation, she, along with our honored king and queen, was assassinated in cold blood by those they trusted most.

"I fear we lost some measure of our honor since that betrayal. I'm afraid our compassion, our kindness, our very joy, died with that young girl. Those of my order had been separated from her for so very long when that tragedy occurred.

"As the regent Balisarius gained influence, our ability to protect her was less and less. All that remained by that time were the memories we were given upon our creation. I know of the Motherworld, have memories, yet have never been there. We were given what we needed to fulfill our duties and nothing more."

Sam looked up at Jimmy and rose to her feet. She held a knotted crown of white and yellow. "I think it lives in you. It's getting dark. I should head home for supper."

"Yes, your family must not worry where you are."

Sam shook her head. "Don't have any. It's just me now." She placed the flowers on his head. Her fingertips from one hand gently glided down his left cheek. She gave him a warm smile in the dimming light before walking home. Jimmy watched her leave while placing his own hand where she had touched him. All the lights on his faceplates glowed red, a flush of something deep within that sparked his circuits. He didn't want to go back to the camp with the soldiers. His existence had been nothing but camp and war. The wilderness called to him.

The din from the longhouse could only be described as emotional chaos, with the bodies of Sindri and his wife covered and laid in the center for people to pay their respects. However, there was more heated debating going on. It was a far cry from the revelry of the previous night. Greta, the uraki breeder, glared at Gunnar and stabbed her finger toward him. "This is your fault, Gunnar."

He shook his head, looking at his feet to avoid the accusatory stares filled with rage. But it was their fear that made the room have the heaviness of black smoke. "I didn't know that he would kill them. I sold that grain fair and square like I would to anyone else. There was no subterfuge or political agenda. The Motherworld never crossed my mind, only the prosperity of our people," said Gunnar with sincerity but no confidence. His face, his voice, his body language all betrayed his feelings: he was a broken man. The room burst into fresh debate. Kora observed and listened.

"Doesn't matter. He's dead now," roared a voice in the crowd.

"It's all his fault," another chimed in.

"What are we gonna do about the soldiers in the granary, yeah? Next it's gonna be the other house." The rabble continued to rouse.

"We'll be slaughtered!" another panicked voice declared.

"Stop! Stop, stop, please," a voice boomed, with more authority and calmness than the rest. It was Den. "How about we bring in the crop and we fall on their mercy? We make ourselves invaluable to them. They wouldn't be able to kill us. They would need us."

"We could stand and fight!" roared Hagen.

Clashing voices spoke at once after he said this. Both Den and Hagen debated others firing questions at Hagen.

Kora took a deep breath and spoke loud enough for everyone to hear her clearly. "No. You cannot fight. Not them. If you have any sense you'll take what you can carry and run."

"And give in? Surrender everything we have lived and worked hard for?" said Greta.

Kora didn't back down. "Everything but your lives. And if I'm being honest, some will give that as well no matter what you do."

Torvald, the ale brewer, slapped a table hard. "I will not leave! My father would kill me for abandoning his legacy. We have been here for generations."

"I refuse to go, too!" cried Hanna.

Den looked around the room then back at Kora. "They are right. This place is all we know. Our history. We cannot leave it for them to destroy. But what about we put our heads down, bring in the crop, and fall on their mercy. We make ourselves invaluable to them. They won't be able to kill us; they'll need us."

"If you submit to them, you become their slaves in every way."

Greta shot Kora an acrimonious glance. "He's right. Farming, that is our skill... that we can do, that they cannot. If we show them how good we are they will be forced to spare us."

Den nodded as Greta spoke. "Do we agree? Our work fights for us."

Kora stood alone with the other villagers fenced around her. She placed a hand on Den's shoulder then let it slip off. "You will do what you want."

"Our work fights for us. Yes?"

Weak but optimistic murmurs rallied in support of Den. No one said the obvious. It was possible that Noble didn't have a trace of humanity in him. If he did, no one had seen it. The weapons and ships were previously unseen by the villagers, but Noble was the truest surprise. They had never met a man like him and they were still too scared to realize the bottomless depths of his inhumanity. Kora understood. It was that understanding that prevented her from looking Den in the eye.

"It's settled then," Den said. "We show them how valuable we are. And when we have fulfilled our side of the deal, they will be forced to rethink how much food they leave us. We can appeal to those gentlemen in the granary, a—appeal to their humanity. How bad can they be?"

Before walking out of the longhouse, Kora paused in front of Gunnar, who had remained silent the entire time. There was nothing but sorrow and confusion on both their faces when their eyes met as she passed. When out of the longhouse, Kora looked toward the sky as she considered her options. She would get out of the village and try to find a way off this planet. It would be easier to escape with only a few soldiers left here and not an army.

. . .

Kora stood in the center of Hagen's house. She had so little to pack it would be an easy journey. This thought left her feeling bitter. Trapped in a vicious cycle. Another move, another temporary bed. She was so sure of this not happening another time. Did peace and joy actually exist, or was it something that would allude her in this life? She began to pack. The nightshirt given to her by Hagen was first.

A familiar creak made her turn around. Hagen stood in the doorway with the setting sun giving him an angelic glow. "So, it's running. Would have thought you'd have had enough of that."

"You heard them. They're delusional. They think those soldiers will show them mercy even after what they did to Sindri, right in front of them," Kora said.

"When I found you in the wreckage of that ship, I considered leaving you. I was afraid you could bring trouble to us. But do I for a moment regret bringing you into our lives? I do not. You've become a part of us. And yet now you leave when we need you most. When your people need you."

A single tear slid down her cheek. She wiped it with the back of her hand and turned away from Hagen. "I can't…"

"You mean, you won't." Hagen shuffled next to her so she couldn't avoid him or this conversation.

She gripped his arthritic, calloused hand. "This place is already lost."

He crooked his head to look her in the eyes. "But what

if that could change? What if we did fight, not only us, but others?"

"Who? Who else do you think would come here and fight?"

"Others that have reason to hate all that the Motherworld represents. Kora, you know this universe better than I. What if you could find the warriors that Noble seeks, the outlaws, to fight alongside us?"

Kora stopped her packing and met his gaze. "If I find warriors to fight for Veldt, I give the village hope. If I give them hope, they fight, and surely lose. I won't have that blood on my hands, nor will I throw my life away the same as the rest of you. I'm sorry, Hagen. I guess you were wrong about me." Kora took the nightshirt out of her leather satchel, placing it on the bed, and walked out the door.

Hagen remained still as she left. "I don't think I was."

It was a short walk to the stables with no one in sight. That was good. She didn't want to explain herself again or say goodbye to people who would be dead soon enough. Goodbyes are easiest when you don't bother. The Realm ensured there were no winners but the Realm. By morning she would be long gone. She would saddle up a uraki and let it lead her far away from here. Anywhere that the Imperium wasn't would be good. The uraki kicked up hay and snorted as she tied the saddle to it. Then a scream broke the silence in the distance. It was a woman. Kora stopped for a moment. As she moved her hand to continue to buckle the last straps, there was another shout, female and male. Kora closed her eyes. *It's no longer your business. You warned them. Go. Go now. You don't owe anyone anything.*

Something crashed, followed by another cry. *Fuck.* Kora dropped her satchel and rushed out of the stables. From a distance she could see the two soldiers and Sam. A knot of anger and frustration formed in her stomach. She turned away and took a few steps behind one of the houses. With her back against the wall, she squeezed her eyes shut, trying to forget the images from her childhood, then the many war campaigns, where that was a common sight to be ignored. But it was Sam. Her friend. Kora leaned the back of her head against the wall and punched the back of her balled fist against the cold stone behind her. She didn't have a choice, she had to leave. Her eyes caught an axe lodged in a wood stump.

Striations of dark blue begin to fill the sky as the sun made way for night. Sam left the river to head home. The path took her past the granary. Marcus and Faunus stood outside, finishing a pipe and picking their teeth from their meal.

"Check this," Marcus said to Faunus. "Hey, water girl. Come here," said Marcus with heavy eyes from an afternoon drinking ale. They demanded most of the barrels in storage be brought to the granary, and food be prepared for the evening.

Sam slowed her pace. "What is it? Did you need some more water?"

"Just a… a little water."

Sam bit her lip and glanced around the empty field. She approached with cautious steps, wishing Jimmy, or one of the villagers, was close. Kora was the first outsider she had met. And Kora was wonderful. This didn't feel right. Marcus had a jug in his hand. She stopped at a safe distance from them but noticed Faunus coming closer to her. "Do you want more? I am heading home, but you can help yourself to the water near the granary. The river is clean," she said, while looking to her left. Faunus was right next to her and moving behind her. She had no choice but to step closer to Marcus. Running was not an option with both so close and not knowing what they might do next.

"I said come here!" Marcus shouted while tossing the jug to the ground. He attempted to grab both her wrists.

"Stop it!" screamed Sam as she ripped away from him.

Marcus's face twisted in contempt and fury. "Or what?" He raised his hand and backhanded her across the face. She would have fallen to the ground if Faunus hadn't caught her, laughing while grabbing her hips.

"Help! Help! Please, help! Help! Get off me!" Sam pleaded as loud as she could to get the attention of someone, anyone in the village.

Marcus used his large palm to ball most of her hair into his hand, and began to drag her toward the granary. "Shut up!"

Faunus laughed while helping Marcus lead her away as she kicked and shouted for help.

"Help me!" she pleaded.

"Shut up!" Marcus said. "Grab her. Let's go. Shut up."

Both men threw her to the ground. She scrambled to get up. "No. Please. Please! Someone help me, please! Please, help! Help me! Get off of me!" From her periphery she saw someone else. It was the youngest soldier who stood up to them before, when they taunted Jimmy for no reason. He jumped up from sitting on a barrel and ran in front of her with his arms outstretched. Even in this stance, his size didn't compare to theirs.

"Don't. Don't," said Aris.

Marcus looked at him with contempt. "That a boy. What do you have in mind?"

Aris leapt toward Marcus, swinging, with eyes incandescent with anger. He managed to land a solid punch to his nose. Marcus stumbled, touching the bridge. He glanced around at the three soldiers seated playing cards or fiddling with weapons. "To your feet. Let's show this snot-nosed prince his place!" shouted Marcus.

A few soldiers heeded his command, dropping whatever they were doing to attack Aris. The young man moved with agility and ferocity, effortlessly dodging the artless attempt from the first soldier who lumbered toward him. The ham-fisted soldier tripped over his own feet when Aris landed a swift punch to his ribs, followed by his back to hit the kidneys. He fell to the ground with the wind knocked out of him and clutching his waist. The others watched in surprise before taking another crack at subduing Aris.

Another rushed toward him only to receive a

roundhouse kick to the face, knocking him off his feet. Blood sprayed from his mouth and a tooth flew through the air. The third soldier grabbed a large wrench from a crate and ran toward Aris with it raised high. As the soldier approached, Aris crouched on the ground to sweep his legs. Shocked, the soldier crashed to the floor, letting go of the wrench in the process. The sudden fall winded him, the wrench landed on him to add injury to injury.

The two other soldiers rose from the ground, recovered from their blows. They ran toward Aris at once with renewed energy. The bloody-mouthed soldier, missing a tooth, retrieved the wrench and swung at Aris. Aris jumped back to avoid the blow, right into the other soldier's range. The angry soldier landed an uppercut. Slightly dazed, Aris put his guard up. Spurred on by finally landing a punch, the soldier dug two shots to Aris's liver. Aris kept backing up. He looked behind him to see how much room he had, and that's when the other soldier swung the wrench. Aris gritted his teeth in pain as the third soldier scrambled to his feet and grabbed him by the neck. He held Aris in a chokehold while the two others stretched his arms out. Marcus walked over and sneered while looking Aris in the eyes. Sam tried to run, but Faunus kicked her in the stomach before standing next to her to prevent her from running again. She cried softly, doubled over.

Marcus stepped closer to Aris. Blood trickled from his nose and onto his lips. He licked it, then balled a fist. "Don't ever try me again, boy." The uppercut took the wind from Aris, who coughed hard after. The room of soldiers erupted in laughter. Marcus kneeled next to Sam, his eyes still on Aris. He grabbed her by the hair again and pulled her head backwards. He licked her cheek then bit her earlobe. Aris struggled to free himself, watching this. She squeezed her eyes shut. Marcus licked her cheek again. "I'm gonna tie you to a post and make you watch every day as she turns from farm girl to whore."

Aris tried to fight against the men holding him. He couldn't get loose. His eyes fell on Sam. Their eyes locked with desperation.

Faunus kicked Marcus in the leg in jest. "Marcus, my good man… This all sounds nice, but you're not gonna do anything… not until I split this sapling myself. Then you may have her. Then you can all have her."

More laughter filled the granary. It echoed against the cold stone.

"Get off her!" Aris cried out.

Faunus stood above Sam and began to unbuckle his belt. "Stop!"

The soldiers looked back to see Kora with chin tilted to her chest and a glare of determination in her eyes as she stared right at them. She held a large axe.

"The second course… perfect. Take her!" shouted Faunus.

Kora sized up the situation with her eyes darting around the room. Her index finger tapped the axe handle with that familiar tingle of annihilation of one's enemy coming over her. In a split second, she wondered if she still possessed the instinct of a precise killer that didn't hesitate to drop a body. One of the most brutal aspects of her training was kill efficiency. The more that fall, the higher the score. She earned her place at the top. With superhuman precision, she clocked every weapon and the position of every target. One of the soldiers had his weapon aimed at her as he approached with his other arm outstretched and palm upright. He flicked his fingers toward himself. She extended the axe handle as if she was about to surrender it to him.

"That's a good girl. Come show us what you have for us. You look like you can take a lot," spat Marcus.

The soldier reached for the axe handle with a slow and steady hand. When he curled his fingers around the wood, she flashed a short smile. In a whirlwind of movement, she pulled the soldier still gripping the axe toward her. Before he could react, she broke his arm by pulling the heavy axe handle from his hand and whacking it across his elbow joint. Before he could drop his gun in the opposite hand, she snatched it from his loose grip. He screamed out, his forearm a mangled dangling rag of flesh. The bone protruded from where his elbow should have been. His screams were silenced when Kora sliced the axe across his neck. His body dropped with a cascade of blood flowing from his throat.

She spun toward cover behind a crate. The men holding Aris let him go to pursue Kora. Taking expert aim without hesitation or thought, she discharged her weapon three times into the missing-toothed soldier's chest and head. Arcs of blood sprayed across the room, but Kora had no time to admire her work as the two other soldiers shot in her direction. She ducked again to check the ammunition in the weapon. As the soldiers neared the crate, she held the gun in her right hand and gripped the axe with the left. When the footfalls sounded close enough, she jumped to her feet, flinging the axe into the midsection of the soldier closest to her whilst shooting her weapon toward the soldier to her left. Both bodies collapsed, making the floor slick with pooling blood.

Aris dashed to the ground to search for a fallen weapon and tried to scramble closer to Sam, but Faunus had her hair in one hand and the other around her neck. Kora grabbed a rifle and blasted the last of the soldiers between the eyes.

Faunus watched Marcus fall and bleed out onto the ground. His head whipped toward Aris, who looked like he had aged ten years in those few seconds. Faunus looked back at Kora. He lifted Sam to his feet and held her in front of his body like a true coward, to make her a human shield.

"Please," Sam said.

"Let her go!" shouted Aris, with a gun pointed at Faunus, who now had his own weapon pointed at Sam's temple.

Faunus looked to Kora, who also pointed her weapon at him. "I will kill her. Is that what you want? Huh? Huh?"

Amidst the stand-off three, heavy stomps neared the entrance of the granary. A metallic creak took their attention to the doorway. They waited to see who would emerge.

Faunus appeared relieved. "About fucking time. Kill her! Kill them both!"

Jimmy's metal face, still crowned with Sam's flowers, twisted toward each of them then paused. He bent down and took one of the discarded weapons in hand but didn't aim it at anyone. He looked at it as if it was a foreign object he didn't know how to use or had long forgotten.

"What are you waiting for? I gave you an order. Fucking kill this b—"

Kora swung her weapon toward Jimmy. In a moment too fast for anyone to react, Faunus's head jolted back, and his body followed. Jimmy's weapon pointed in his direction. Blood dripped from the side of Sam's face. She trembled, still unable to move despite being free from a dead Faunus. She looked up at Jimmy with relief and tears welling in her eyes.

The robot dropped the weapon and fled into the darkness. His heavy steps faded as he ran. Kora turned back to Aris, who held up one hand while putting his weapon down. She also lowered her weapon, seeing he meant her no harm. Aris wasted no time rushing to Sam, who was sobbing as she hugged herself. Aris wrapped an arm around her and wiped the blood from the side of her face with his hand. Sam melted into his arms.

Kora took in the carnage, breathing hard and letting the axe slide from her hand. This was a scene she knew intimately. It had found her again, like a rabid, vicious animal. This was the violence that accompanied invasion, subjugation. The ground that usually remained spotless for grain was littered with blood, with pieces of scattered flesh. The crunching of rocks underfoot broke her thoughts. In an instant, she swung around toward the entrance with weapon in hand. Someone approached.

She remained ready for another fight. Her breathing and heart raced in anticipation.

It was Den, followed by a handful of villagers. Gasps and whispers of shock were all they could muster. Den searched her face, wet with sweat and blood, his own face reflecting his utter confusion.

Kora lowered her weapon. "We're gonna have to fight."

Hagen broke through the crowd. He stared at the dead soldiers, then back to Kora and Sam's torn dress. Tears still spilled from the young woman's eyes. He nodded his head. "We need to build a pyre. A large one. Strip the bodies then burn them all."

Den placed a hand on his shoulder, but kept his eyes on Kora before turning to the villagers. "You heard him. Let's get to work and clean this up."

Sam turned to Aris. "Thank you."

He shook his head. "Jimmy had the shot. Not me."

"No, but you stopped them. You stood up for me. You'll be in trouble now."

Aris watched the villagers drag the dead soldiers out of the granary, their blood leaving track marks on the ground. "I was never one of them and never could be. I couldn't save my family. At least now I can try to… I don't know. Maybe make up for it all."

"Well, you can't stay in here tonight. You can stay at mine."

He gave her a kind smile. "Thank you. I'd appreciate that.

THE SUN SEEMED TO RISE FASTER THAN OTHER MORNINGS. NO ONE SLEPT. The soldiers were tossed into the fire and the granary was cleaned. Their weapons and uniforms were kept in the corner. Den continued to give out orders to make the village appear normal again. Hagen left the granary, then returned to Kora with a folded, cream-colored Veldtian linen in his hands. "Kora, you may need this. I found it at the site of the crash."

Kora took the parcel from him. It had weight and the shape was familiar. She unwrapped the first layer. "I thought it was lost." Her eyes widened.

"Our culture is not for such weapons. I feared it could be dangerous."

Kora's fingertips ran across a leather holster and Guardian Gun. She touched the gold filigree that plated the outside. In script that matched the design were the engraved words: *My Life for Hers*. This was the beautiful deliverer of death that never left her side for years. It was a gift from the king for her service to their family. She agreed to protect the princess with it at all costs. "You were right. Thank you."

Kora handed the linen back to Hagen then inspected the pistol to see if it had any visible damage. Her fall from the sky, and grace, had not been an easy one. She holstered it, satisfied with the condition.

"Where will you go?" asked Hagen.

"There is someone, a general named Titus. Once a hero of the Realm who turned his own forces against those of the Motherworld. Last I heard, he was still out there somewhere. If I could find him, and men for him to lead…"

Hagen hugged Kora, and she wrapped her arms around him.

When their embrace ended, she looked at the exhausted villagers getting ready to return to their homes. She saw Gunnar in the distance on his own, not speaking to anyone. They had kept their distance from him for the last few hours with glares of suspicion. Some grumbled beneath their breath. He did his best to ignore them and help clean up the mess, but couldn't help looking lost and confused.

"Gunnar," she called out as she walked toward him.

He lifted his head. Up close it looked like he hadn't slept in days.

"Last year, in Providence, you sold grain to the resistance."

He glanced at the villagers watching him closely before

lowering his voice. "Yes. I met a man there who introduced me to the insurgents. The Bloodaxes."

"Would he still know how to find them?"

He shook his head and shrugged. "It's possible."

Kora only knew Gunnar to be honest with her. "Then you'll take me to him?"

Gunnar looked up and shifted his weight. The villagers talked amongst themselves in hushed voices. He seemed agitated, but not at Kora. He looked her in the eyes and stepped closer to her. "Of course I will."

The villagers' voices grew louder, expressing suspicion and disdain toward him.

"Hey! Bring down one more uraki!" Gunnar said.

"We leave now. Grab what you need," said Kora, as she turned to head to the stables. Gunnar rushed past her to gather his belongings. The villagers continued to watch him run, then turned their gaze toward Kora, who continued on her path.

"Kora."

She looked back to see Den jogging toward her. He appeared tired, but not spent. The man did have stamina and grit. "You aren't going to say goodbye? You have proved you can take care of yourself, but it's still dangerous."

Kora glanced to see if Gunnar was returning yet. "Hopefully it isn't goodbye. I'd like to live a few more years."

His body moved slightly toward her, but then he hesitated and remained where he was. "Be safe out there. Come back." Sincerity shined in his eyes, but Kora knew it could not go beyond his bed.

"Thank you. Keep them safe." She turned and continued toward the stables. Maybe sex with him was a big mistake, or it could have been the last time before she died. Either way, what was done was done.

In the stables, she put on her holster and a long tan cloak to hide it. Her skills and intentions were on a need-to-know basis. The beasts seemed well fed and watered before the journey, which was good, because they had to make as much distance toward Providence as they could.

The bag she packed the night before was still tied to the saddle on her uraki. Gunner dashed into the stables, out of breath and red-faced. He saddled another one of the uraki with his own supplies. He paused when he finished and looked to Kora.

Kora untied her uraki and began to lead it out of the stables, and gave him a smile. She didn't want to make any promises either, because this was like no other fight she had ever encountered. Both mounted outside the stables as Hagen approached alone. "A general, and an army? We might stand a chance."

Kora smiled at Hagen, who seemed more cheerful and optimistic than her. "I make no promises. But we will try." She glanced back Gunnar.

"One more thing before you leave. Is there anything on the ship you came in that could help us?"

Kora paused and thought for a moment. "The guns. The ship is definitely useful if it's working."

Hagen nodded and looked despondent.

"Why don't you ask that young soldier who helped us?" Kora suggested. "He is obviously no friend to the Imperium, and if they find out what he did, it will mean his death for treason."

"That's a great idea. A safe journey to the both of you."

Kora gave him one last short smile and pulled on the leather reins, and heeled the uraki. Gunnar followed her lead. Neither looked back at the villagers gathered to watch their only hope disappear over the horizon. They would travel through the forested mountains until it got dark.

The small fire had died down enough for the light of the stars to be seen better. Kora and Gunnar made camp when they couldn't safely travel any longer. With decent weather at this time of year, they traveled a good distance before stopping. The only sounds were the heavy breaths and snorts from the sleeping uraki and firewood breaking apart. Once settled on their bedrolls, both Gunnar and Kora stared at the sky. Kora had her pistol right next to her.

Gunnar finally relieved himself of the question he'd had on his mind. "So you were a soldier for the Motherworld? Fighting for the Realm?"

"You could say that," said Kora, without looking at Gunnar.

"Of high rank, I suppose?"

Gunnar's question was only met with the crackling of embers.

"I mean..." he continued. "Are you wanted for desertion?"

Kora smiled and chuckled. "That and more."

"Okay."

"Anything else you wanna ask me?"

Gunnar paused before turning on his side to face Kora. "They won't just kill us, will they? I mean, I understand making an example of Sindri to keep us in line, but we're just farmers, we're not a threat. How can you know they will destroy us?"

She remained on her back, staring into the darkness. "When they first came to my world, I was nine years old. They never asked for anything, there were no terms. Only the lust for destruction."

Kora had to stay inside. That is what she remembered when she woke up. Her mother seemed unusually tense and was not working downstairs. She didn't ask Kora to get dressed or help around the house. She paced and looked through the drawn curtains in their modest apartment above the tea shop they owned. But Kora's father was in and out of the apartment with her two older siblings.

Her father burst through the door with a look of panic before slamming it shut.

"We have to go… now! We will head to the forest on the outskirts and hopefully meet up with others. The caves should give us some protection. They go pretty deep, much deeper if you don't know them." He rushed to the locked wardrobe in the front room and removed his rifle he sometimes used for hunting. Kora's mother turned to her. "Grab only what you can carry." Large booms exploded overhead, followed by screams and shouts in the distance.

"I thought we would have more time," her father said with genuine despair in his eyes. "Our people are doing their best to fight back." Their house shook and the smell of fire and charred flesh permeated the atmosphere. It wafted through an open window. "Sounds like they are getting closer," he said as he gripped his rifle tighter. The fighting seemed to be just outside their door. Kora's mother stopped her packing for a moment. "What could they possibly want?"

He looked her dead in the eyes, with every muscle in his face sagging from fear and exhaustion. "Everything."

Her mother glanced at her. "Go to your room and get ready to go. If it sounds too scary, I want you to stay in your room then go straight for the forest. Your brother and sister should be back any minute now. They are securing the shop."

Kora nodded and obeyed her mother. She shut the door and grabbed the bag her sister gave her for her previous birthday. It was hand stitched with her name at the top. A vicious explosion hit their building. Kora could hear her mother scream and a window break. Kora dropped to her knees and covered her ears. But it was not enough to drown out the shouts of strange men and her parents.

Her brother and sister pleaded with the unfamiliar voices. Then multiple shots. Silence. Kora's little heart thumped. She rose to her feet and walked to the door, opening it a crack. She continued into the main room and stopped. Her family went quiet because they were dead.

She looked at her parents' blood sprayed against the wall above the sofa, her brother and sister crumpled on the ground near the dining table. She was glad she didn't see it happen, but having to acknowledge they were dead was worse. Kora couldn't pull her eyes away from them until heavy footfalls hit the stairs. Kora remained still, not able to register what to do. Shock paralyzed her.

A soldier whose face was covered with his battle gear sized her up before moving on to more screams in the building. Another explosion made her look out of the shattered window. There were no clouds or sunlight to be seen that day. Only warships, dropships firing at will, and smoke. The wails of the few survivors cut through the sounds of falling buildings and brutal fighting.

Kora turned and walked out without looking at her family again. Soldiers poured in and out of the building, their weapons aimed at anything that moved. Her neighbor thrashed her legs while being pulled by the hair then thrown to the ground by two soldiers. The woman who always bought their tea, and sometimes came to the apartment to gossip about the other tenants, now pleaded for her life as the soldiers ripped her dress. Kora ran faster down the stairs and into the chaos on the street.

Bodies lay where they fell. Viscera and blood saturated the ground. She hesitated to go farther, seeing a group of people from the town pointing long-range pulse pistols and heat signature rifles to the sky. The staccato of rapid fire overhead made her cover her ears again. Each of those people fell dead with multiple shots to their bodies. There was no way to outrun whatever killed them. When the threat was gone, she began to move again, but a pistol in the hands of a bloating dead man caught her eye.

He stared with his mouth and eyes open and a large blast to his chest. The bleeding had stopped as decay began to settle in and flies circled. Kora hesitated with trepidation, feeling scared of seeing another dead body up close. But her fear of the invaders scared her more. Her mother and father showed her a few times their own pistol they had at the tea shop for would-be thieves. It wasn't exactly the same, but maybe it would work. She kneeled and slowly outstretched her hand, then snatched it as quickly as possible to avoid being close to the dead man.

She scrambled through the back alleys, ducking behind demolished buildings and abandoned vehicles as gunfire and cannon fire lit up the sky and filled the atmosphere with the deafening sounds of war. The shadows and lights of warships cast their gaze across the city. Bloodcurdling screams and shouts of soldiers and citizens made her want to cry, but that wouldn't get her closer to the possible safety of the forest. She hoped there was some sanctuary left.

She breathed hard, her heart thumped from running faster than she ever had in her life, despite not knowing what could be around the next corner. When she entered a parade of shops in Vega Square, she had to dash behind an abandoned fruit stall. She waited for advancing troops to clear and needed a rest. Her small body wanted to collapse.

"I understand your pain, your fear, your loss. My name is Balisarius. Who are you?"

He cradled her small hands, still on the gun and finger on the trigger, whilst kneeling in front of her. Their eyes locked in a stand-off of fire and agony.

"Kora," she whispered.

"Set me free, child, you can do it. I know you can… please." Balisarius placed the barrel of the gun to his forehead and closed his eyes.

Her breathing increased and her whimpers released tears that fell on their hands holding the gun. Kora squeezed the trigger. It only fired a hollow click. Balisarius opened his eyes wide and shuddered, seeing the terror in her eyes. He seemed to like that she pulled the trigger. Her entire body shook before her eyes fluttered and she collapsed into his arms. He stared at her filthy face and moved sweaty strands of hair away from her eyes. "I think you shall be called Arthelais. You will scarcely remember this life or city." Without effort he rose to his feet with Kora in his arms, and walked back to the entrance of the alley. The fighting was dying down and his dropship awaited to return to the Motherworld and receive congratulations. This small prize would be a gift to himself and his legacy. Every leader had an heir.

Kora awoke on a large bed in a sparse room with no art or pictures. There was a window looking out into the darkness of space. Her home could no longer be seen. The sheets were clean and smelled of chemicals. Next to the bed a large glass of cold water sweated on a tray that also held a bowl of fresh cut fruit. A partition door snapped open. The sound made her jump. It was the man she had pointed the gun at.

"You are awake. I hope you feel better."

Kora nodded. His eyes shifted toward the tray. "Please eat and drink. We have a long journey ahead of us. You will need your strength."

"Where are you taking me?" she asked.

He sat at the edge of the bed. "A place called Moa, the Motherworld. It will be your new home… with me."

"Why?" Her wide eyes surveyed him. He no longer had blood on him or looked like a soldier.

"This is not a time for questions, but for gratitude. I want to give you what very few like you ever get."

Kora's head dropped and she began to cry. "Please don't hurt me."

He edged closer and lifted her chin. "Never. That is not my intention. You will see that."

He wiped her tears with his hand. "When we get to the Motherworld, I will have time to show you what a splendid place it is. You will learn amazing things about the universe and the Realm."

Kora's belly rumbled loud enough for them both to hear. He smiled at her. "Why don't you eat? You will feel better. And sleep. After, I can show you around this ship."

Her little body shuffled closer to the side table. She

grabbed the fork and took a bite of melon. The taste made her grab more, forgetting her fear as she shoveled it into her mouth.

"See, isn't that better? You are perfectly safe now."

Kora turned to him and nodded and swallowed. "Thank you."

"I will be in the other room, but I can see in here. If you need anything, just wave and I will be right in. That door to your left is a bathroom. There are fresh clothes, probably too big, and you can take a bath if you like. No one can see in there. Then I would like you to sleep."

Kora didn't want to say no. Where else would she have gone, and what would have become of her? Even though this was a room on a ship, it felt like a palace. She wondered if they would go to a real palace.

Balisarius stood. "I know you are a good girl. You will learn to love the Motherworld and our king just as I do. Do you know about the king?"

She shook her head.

"That will be something we can work on. But for now, I want you to eat and have a nice bath." He gave her another smile before walking out the partition door through which he'd entered.

When he was gone, she hopped off the bed and into the bathroom. It was just as simple as the bedroom. She rushed to the black clothes. She unfolded the top that was too large, but it looked like it was part of a pajama set. It had no design or writing. Her hand reached for the bath's faucet. Hot water gushed out smoothly.

No pinging from shared pipes in a crowded building or waiting for it to heat up. Her siblings shouting at her for taking all the hot water. The guilt of still being alive clung to her with the stench of the dead that lay in her destroyed city.

Her heart felt broken. She didn't want to take a bath or eat sweet fruit. She began to cry again, remembering the sight of her dead parents staring at her with their brains splashed against the wall. Steam filled the room with the hot water still running. The thought of her parents made her body tense. She had to take a bath and eat her fruit.

What if he got mad and had her killed, too? Maybe the soldiers who did that were on another part of this ship. Kora made the water the right temperature before rushing to undress and get into the water. She lay back and imagined this would be okay. Why would he give this to her if he didn't mean well?

After the bath, she dressed in her too-large clothes and got back into bed. She felt drowsy and warm. Without realizing it, her eyes closed.

Balisarius watched the child fall asleep. He hoped he had gained her trust and she felt more at ease. At her age she should bounce back easily, especially once she saw the Motherworld and all it could offer her. He had to come up with a plan to seamlessly bring her into his life and life in the royal court without anyone objecting to it. Her name, identity, home world, all of it had to be erased, a phantom memory. Her new life would replace the old and her loyalty would be unwavering to him and the Realm. Every part of his life had to be perfect.

Kora became his shadow as she grew from a child, with her hair cut bluntly at her shoulders and across her forehead, to a young woman. She was exposed to the art of the Motherworld. There was no expense spared in her education. She stood next to Balisarius when the noble families of Veii kneeled before him. Balisarius wore his best uniform and Kora a smaller version of the uniform made especially for the visit to Veii. "Get used to people at your feet," he said in her ear. Kora didn't know what he meant, but she also didn't want to ask. He gave her a new life outside of war and so she remained obedient as if he were her father. The memory of her biological family faded year by year.

The trip to Veii was uneventful until it was time to leave. With the Veii noble's heads bowed in submission and the terms of surrender secured, he and his guard surrounded them with weapons aimed. All entrances were blocked. Kora stood next to her adopted father, not knowing what to feel or think. She gripped the hem of her jacket to keep from shaking. A girl, not much older than Kora, lifted her gaze to her with tears in her eyes that seemed to call for help. Kora stared at her back and bit her lip. As the Imperium soldiers moved toward the nobility, Kora's eyes darted across the crowd, who began to look around in confusion. Kora's face went hot with an anxious fear rising from her stomach to her cheeks. She felt just as confused. Balisarius must have noticed, because he took hold of Kora's hand before lifting the other and bringing it down like a gavel. Without any chance to escape, or warning, the soldiers fired. Kora watched, unable to show any emotion as the girl her age fell to the floor with her body bouncing uncontrollably from the storm of bullets hitting flesh. Every single noble lay dead.

Balisarius turned to Kora with tears in his eyes. "Now, my daughter, *your* training will begin. If anyone can succeed, it will be you. Don't let me down. I will miss you so very much."

After that incident, Kora wandered through the boiler and engine rooms. She walked along a metal walkway above the furnaces. Before her was a giant metal encasement, in the shape of a nude woman kneeling with her hands bound behind her back and pulled toward the top of the room. Her torso and head faced down. Thick tubes of red energy surged into her open mouth. Tubes of blue energy almost like hair emerged from the crown of her head and connected to the room. Kora walked close enough to touch the metal face. Something was alive in there.

A "Kali", she had heard it called. Kora closed her eyes. She allowed her sorrow to rise to the surface. In that moment, she could feel whatever was trapped inside felt it too. Her entire body buzzed with the being's energy. Then it opened its eyes. Kora looked deep within then bowed her head. She was not the only one feeling alone and trapped. Kora turned to walk back to her room, feeling like someone on that ship understood what she had been through.

Years later, Kora was sent to the elite Imperium military academy not far from the capital. She had never seen so many who hailed from different worlds. They wore the same uniforms, and those in new armor glowed with the light of the heavens as they marched. She wondered if they were all like her, orphans of pillaging and plundering. But Balisarius always made it clear she couldn't tell anyone about her past or where she came from. It didn't matter. She belonged to the Home World, and she belonged here, just like him.

She would become greater than she ever could living in a cramped apartment selling tea. What kind of life was that? Her parents' death was a blessing because it gave birth to her new life. A better life. This was their secret. One thing she knew for certain was she had to be the best. When she entered the spartan, nondescript building for the Registration Authority, a scribe dressed all in red approached her. His face was veiled like the priests'. Kora stepped forward. "I am Arthelais."

"I know. Your identity was scanned when you walked past the threshold. Now, we already have your clothing and shoe size. But first you must have your hair shorn."

Kora touched the ends of her long locks, then looked at the plain recruit uniform in the scribe's hands as he placed it on the long stone reception desk. Balisarius's words on Veii rang in her ears with the image of the slaughtered nobles bleeding on the floor. *Don't let me down.*

"May I ask what to expect?"

"No. You will learn to adapt and do as you're told when you are told. Proceed through those doors. Then you will be told where you will sleep for the duration of this phase of training."

"Thank you," said Kora, before taking her uniform off the desk and leaving to have her hair cut in the same short fashion as everyone else. So far, it didn't seem too bad, but nothing could prepare her for what lay in wait.

After years of grueling physical training in every conceivable environment, and combat training that left her with broken bones, she was molded into what she hated, the perfect killing machine. Her last test before graduation was the most brutal and soul-breaking. At the top of her class, with the highest scores, she was given an assignment others did not receive. Her superior handed her a pistol in the training pit usually reserved for hand-to-hand combat practice. The sandy ground was soft underfoot. "Arthelais, I have been told to inform you Balisarius wishes you the best of luck today. He knows you will pass this without issue."

Kora nodded and waited. She didn't know what to expect, holding a pistol far from the shooting range and weapons hall. No one else was around as it was a fifteen-minute walk, tucked behind the main square used for group training exercises. This was one of many isolated training pods used for smaller lessons. In the distance she could hear a rumbling. It was a closed transport vehicle. It stopped next to them. The doors opened and two academy training leaders pulled out a hooded man. They dragged him into the training pit and pushed him to his knees in the sand.

Kora felt sick. This was the test? Her hand trembled and she swallowed hard. The sun beat harder on her shoulders. She could feel sweat trickle down her neck and from beneath her breasts. She wiped one sweaty palm at a time on her training fatigues. The training leader pulled off the hood from the man's head. His face was bruised and battered, but his eyes could still look into hers, plead with her better nature.

"This man is a traitor. He has been found guilty and is now ready to receive his punishment."

Kora looked at her superior next to her. "What are you asking me to do? What did he do?"

He smiled. "Kora, you are a bright woman. You are the adjudicator of his punishment. Aim your weapon and pull the trigger. And I already told you what he did. He is a traitor. Traitors disobey and cause chaos for the Realm."

She glanced back at the man, who shook his head. "Please don't. They are lying." Tears streamed from his eyes. She checked to see if the weapon was loaded or live. It was in perfect working order. Her superior leaned closer. "This is the final test, Kora. You didn't go this far to fail now." His breath smelled sour and his presence was heavy.

Kora felt her entire body go cold and to stone despite the heat. She had to do this without question or remorse. *Don't let me down.* Balisarius's words returned like the whisper of a ghost. Part of her wondered if he set this up specifically for her to test her loyalty to him. She turned to the man who was now on his knees in front of her. Her arm raised with the pistol in hand. She tried to envision the soldiers who killed her parents and she saw ravaging her neighbor Lanet. Bad men, men who deserved to die.

But when she felt herself pull the trigger, she couldn't help her twisted mind seeing Balisarius and his head exploding from her rage. What would her life have been if the pistol she had on him had discharged? She unloaded three perfect shots to the center of the man's skull. He lay on the ground with his face unrecognizable. Her superior touched her shoulder and extended his hand, palm up. "Well done. I will send the report you are to graduate with top honors. You passed the test. Balisarius will be pleased. You may leave now."

Feeling numb, she placed the pistol back into his hand and left the training pit for the barracks. She didn't want to look back or hear them bundle the body back in the vehicle. Something inside of her had shattered the moment she pulled the trigger. This was her new life, her duty. She went to bed in her private room that night, face down on the pillow. She cried silently and asked the man she had killed but never met for forgiveness, as she wondered if she could ever forgive herself.

Because of her success and high scores, she would be given her own command. Without delay, she would be shipped off somewhere in the universe.

The king addressed the graduating soldiers that day. He stood at the podium with head held high and face glowing like the crown he wore on his head. The crowd cheered as he smiled whilst looking across the graduates all wearing the same uniforms. Behind them were invited guests. Kora saw Balisarius watched from the royal box to the right of the king. He looked as if he was about to give a speech himself. She had not seen him in person since the day she left, only hologram transmissions. Her training was too important to be disrupted by visits. He had big plans for her. Kora's gaze shifted from Balisarius to the king, who raised his hand to silence the crowd.

"The path you forge from this day forward and through the cycles ahead will not be easy. Many of you will give your lives for the greater good, the Realm and all it stands for. Rest assured your sacrifice is appreciated and your death a glorious one. Destiny will welcome you into their halls so long as you have been obedient to your duty, carrying on in the same manner of your ancestors of the Motherworld. Remember their latitude and grace, yet always having a firm hand. In all your eyes I see the nobility and honor we ask of you."

The entire crowd erupted into cheers and threw their caps into the air. Kora's mind felt dislocated from her body. It wandered to her childhood as she looked around at proud family members also celebrating. She remembered the dead girl on Veii who should be finishing her education.

Kora didn't know much about the king, only the work Balisarius carried out on his behalf. Her gaze shifted to Balisarius, who watched the king with tears in his eyes as he clapped. Her adopted father glanced in her direction and gave her a short nod. It crossed her mind she could very well be sent to her death wherever her first post took her. In the crowd of hundreds, she had never felt more alone. But this was her duty and the only life she knew. The better life, she had been told.

She cheered with the rest of the crowd, with an arm pulling her close. She turned to see the lover she had taken, as advised by the Academy. Death stalked Kora; she envisaged the day they'd see each other die, but his touch pushed those thoughts away. He kissed her hard and smiled. She wasn't alone. Until her last day, she would fight like her comrades for the glory of a place that was not her own. When constant war wore the soldiers down, having someone to fight with, to fight for, was the only thing to keep them going.

The fire had diminished to almost nothing by the time Kora finished telling Gunnar part of her life before Veldt.

"You were saved by the Imperium."

Kora finally turned to face Gunnar. "I never knew why, out of all the places they conquered and millions killed, why he spared me. Just to make me one of them. I spent year after year on a warship. No family or inkling of love. Only fighting. War."

"How old were you?"

"I was made an officer and given my own command at eighteen. The things I have seen and was told when I was just a kid. They broke me to make what they needed. That's their way. And there is no room for dissent. All that matters are the ideas and culture of the Motherworld. There is no room for anything else to exist." Kora turned onto her back again and closed her eyes.

"Thank you for telling me this. It means a lot to me."

"I'm only telling you this so you know who I am. You asked how I know they'll destroy you? That's what I would do."

Gunnar continued to watch Kora with only the illumination of embers and starlight. When he saw she wasn't moving, he lay back down to sleep.

It didn't take long to ride into the valley and on to Providence. The city, walled in tightly, clustered buildings of all sizes. Mammoth iron gates at the front served for extra protection. The tiled peaks that winged out of the sides of the squat buildings could just be seen rising above the gates. Some had multiple tiers overlooking the city, with many winding alleyways that served to protect those who wanted to move without being seen. The outer perimeter of the town was reserved for merchants and businesses, while the inner parts were residences.

Residences were simple, as low-profile as possible so as not to tempt criminals. And there were plenty of those brought in for the underbelly of trading. You wouldn't know it at first glance, but Providence was a black-market hub. The planet didn't produce anything remarkable or have valuable natural resources, therefore it was off-radar. The business leaders of Providence formed a council that controlled everything, from maintaining the gates to keeping some sort of peace. Anyone could petition a grievance at the weekly council hearings or slide a little extra coin into palms to turn a blind eye. The priority of the council was to keep the town in a state of consistent prosperity, whether that be legitimate, or not.

There was no enforced curfew or limits on what could be bought or sold. If trouble found you, good luck. Providence was the closest place to get a taste of other worlds or to get off Veldt. Besides the black market, it was used as a trading post or waystation to refuel before moving on. After Providence, the landscape became mountainous and rural again. Wealthy businessowners usually kept a small apartment in the town, their larger, grander homes built on isolated patches of land.

The weather had taken a turn when they arrived at Providence. Rain pelted down from a thunderstorm. As they approached, the gates opened. Gunnar moved his uraki closer to Kora's. "Just want to prepare you. The establishment where we're going—it's a brothel. That's where the contact introduced me to Devra."

Kora's face remained calm. "That's fine. Devra? Your contact is a prostitute?"

"No, nothing like that. Devra is the leader of the Bloodaxes, the outlaws… that I sold the grain to." Gunnar looked down as he trailed off.

The stables were full, but there was some room. Once they'd paid for the uraki to be watered and fed, they made their way to the Crown City Emporium of Pleasure. There was no sign, only oxblood-red doors. It had multiple levels with all windows shuttered. Before they could ring the bell, the doors burst open with a din of noise flooding out into the street. A man even larger than Den ran out and fell to the ground, face first. Two others pursued him from behind. Dressed in their emblematic black and gray uniforms, Kora knew them instantly. Their appearance was as fierce as their reputation. With mottled skin, various colored eyes, sharpened teeth, and noses evolved naturally with a heightened sense of smell, they were known to anyone who laid eyes on them. Gunnar stepped back from the fray.

"They're Hawkshaws. Bounty hunters. They work for the Imperium. A symptom of the presence of our new 'friends'." said Kora as she watched the fight.

One of the Hawkshaws, with a large scar running down his face, kicked the man on the ground in the ribs. He cried out and rolled onto his back in pain.

"Wait. Oh no," Gunnar whispered to Kora.

"What is it?"

"Oh no. Their captive. He's the guy we're coming to

see. The one I thought could help us." Kora and Gunnar watched their contact get pulled from the ground by a four-legged metal constraint that kept him upright but unable to move, as it clamped his ankles, torso, and head to a metal spine. The robotic constraint walked next to the Hawkshaws.

"Did the Bloodaxes give you any other way to contact them?"

Gunnar followed the Hawkshaws and Ximon with his eyes until they were out of sight. He shook his head. "They said they were sheltered on a planet called Sharaan, before they came here, protected by a king named Levitica."

"Levitica," Kora repeated, pausing to think, then stomped toward the brothel, slapping the door open before it closed. "Come," she said. Gunnar followed her without question.

The clash of voices and languages matched the aromas of bodies, alcohol, and heavy smoke. Satisfied clients descended from staircases on the opposite sides of the main floor, wiping sweat and water from their necks and faces. The beat of drums was as hypnotic as the many vices on display. To their left was the flesh auction. A female species with large horns jutting from both sides of her head stood at attention with gold tight ropes tied to her limbs. She wore a metal corset secured with a bolted lock. One key, one buyer. The gold ropes led to a mouthpiece keeping her lips pried open to show the depths of her auto-constricting throat. Her iridescent eyes followed Gunnar.

He met her gaze then quickly looked in the opposite direction as he quickened his pace. Kora appeared more relaxed than him as she walked confidently through. All species, races, and genders could be bought and sold for the right price. The stage glowed with low light overhead. A male and female new to the auction walked on stage with numbers tattooed on their thighs. They wore only enough cloth to cover what was meant for their buyer.

Gunnar shied away from looking at the sex workers for too long and set his gaze on the gambling tables to the right. He glanced at Kora to see if she watched him. Cheers and shouts erupted amongst the winners and losers in the games of chance. Huge, heavily armed bouncers walked around the tables, ready to stop a fight if one occurred. Gunnar avoided them too, not wanting to cause any trouble or bring attention to himself.

There was a long bar at the back. Kora glanced toward Gunnar, who trailed behind, trying to stifle his curiosity. When he had met the Bloodaxes, they had gone through a back door and into a private room. He had missed most of this. He picked up his pace again to keep up with her.

She slid onto a stool. An android bartender behind the bar stopped cleaning metal bowls with two of its many hands and looked at Kora with its yellowed eyes. Its shoulders and back acted as a candelabra, with mounting wax creating a mountain range of flame on its shoulders.

"Carbost," said Kora.

"I'll have what she's having," Gunnar said.

Kora elbowed Gunnar and flicked her head to the right. A Hawkshaw gave a wad of cash to a hooded patron. She tried to get a look at who was behind the hood, but no luck. They didn't want to be seen. This place wasn't just for entertainment. It also gave anyone cover for under-the-table deals. There were too many distractions to notice everyone's business. When the Hawkshaw walked away from the hooded patron at the bar, Kora turned to her awaiting drink.

Gunnar looked suspiciously at the dirty shot glass filled with a murky brown liquid topped with small granules floating to the surface. Kora gulped the drink, unphased by its appearance. Gunnar coughed and winced at its strength when he attempted to drink with the same ease as her. He looked toward the hooded patron again. "I think our best chance to find the Bloodaxes is to contact the Leviticans."

"It might expose us. First, we find General Titus, then we'll see about your rebels."

She glanced at the full shot glass in front of Gunnar. "You gonna drink that?"

"Oh… um… yeah." He lifted the shot glass and drank it in one hit. His eyes squeezed shut and his face twisted. "Delicious," he croaked, trying to stifle a cough as the liquid slid down his throat.

Gunnar's eyes shifted to his left. A stranger with pale pink skin and loose brown-spotted jowls sat next to him. His hairless dog-like face glistened with sweat. Cheap cologne sat on top of thick body odor. He panted softly, which made his rotund belly shake beneath his sweat stained shirt. He scratched the wiry hairs poking from his low-cut shirt. "Is this your owner?"

"Move on. He's not for sale," Kora said.

He sniffed Gunnar. "Everything's for sale in this place, so, how much? You know, I have a room upstairs with relatively clean sheets." He flashed Gunnar a dirty smile that filled him with revulsion and shame.

"No," Gunnar said while recoiling.

The dog-faced man moved closer to Gunnar, putting his body next to his. Gunnar took a step toward Kora with the heat of the stranger's breath on his neck. It smelled like he had been licking his own ass.

"That's a very generous offer. But I don't think so…" Gunnar said as politely as he could.

The dog-faced man growled and reached beneath the bar, squeezing Gunnar's cock and balls in one of his hairy sharp-nailed hands. "I guarantee you, by morning, you're gonna be begging me for more." He stuck out his tongue and waggled it back and forth.

Gunnar stood motionless. Kora took two large strides toward the stranger and smacked his hand away. "I said move on."

His flabby lips and trimmed whiskers formed a scowl. "Come on, Mama. Let him come and play. If you want to keep him that bad, he must be a good fuck."

Kora stood her ground while giving him a hard stare devoid of fear. "You need to leave."

He growled and whipped out a jagged-edged blade

sheathed in a holster attached to his belt. He grabbed Kora by the throat with one hand and placed the knife just below.

"Listen close, you jealous little bitch. I'm gonna fuck that pretty pink hole in his face and there's nothing you can do to stop me."

Without warning and with lightning speed, Kora snatched the knife from his hand then smacked his head against the bar. She held his own knife to his throat. The entire bar went silent with the show. The faintest of sounds could be heard. "No, you listen close. The only one who's about to get fucked in here is you."

Kora kneed him hard in the crotch, causing him to howl and double over in agony. She pushed him to the ground. He crawled through the still silent crowd whimpering. The rest of the patrons and Gunnar continued to watch her as she turned to the bar to order another drink. After downing a second carbost, she turned to see the room hadn't resumed its normal level of activity. She eyed the crowd then marched toward a short stage with a long-legged creature on auction. The tattoo on its thigh was bright red. A wire with a small globe attached to the end hung from the ceiling in the center of the stage. The auctioneer stepped aside for her.

"I'm looking for information. Has anyone here heard of General Titus?"

The room burst into a loud buzz of conversation after this question was asked.

But one voice pierced the tumult. "Of course, General

Titus. Crazy bastard. Turned his own men on the Motherworld's forces at the Battle of Sarawu."

Kora stepped down from the stage and approached a table with a strung-out half-dressed man with shaggy greasy black hair. He sat slumped on a chair like a puppet. His eyes were milky white and focused on nothing. The man was no longer in control of himself or aware of anything. Two thick tentacles that pulsed were lodged to either side of his throat. They were connected to a large slimy blue flea-like creature that was all brain, with a single red eye surrounded by black bristles. The parasite was the size of the man's head and stood on stubby needle-like legs. It wasn't the man who spoke, it was this creature who had no vocal cords of its own. It scuttled on the table next to the puppet human it used to communicate.

"Do you know of his location?" Kora asked. She glanced back, feeling someone close. It was Gunnar.

The tentacles on the man's neck glowed brighter when he spoke, but he remained under complete control of the parasite. "Last I heard, he was fighting in the coliseum at Pollux. I'd be careful if I were you, little miss. Last hunter who went looking for him ended up with his head on a pike outside the coliseum entrance as a warning not to bother him."

"So, he's on Pollux." Kora began to walk out. Gunnar followed closely.

"That's your plan?" he asked.

"That's my plan." She looked at him. "What?"

"Guess we need to find a ship to take us to Pollux."

"You're catching on."

Before they could leave, the pink-faced man had returned. "Hey! Bitch! Oh. You should have killed me! Now you're gonna die."

The dog-faced man had murder and rage in his face. His eyes were yellowed and his mouth dripped with saliva. Kora wasn't fazed by his bravado. She glanced at Gunnar, who took a step back. "I'm gonna give you one chance to just turn and walk away."

He licked his lips. "Uh-oh. Are you gonna give all of us one chance?"

Three thugs with weapons stepped from the shadows, growling low, including one behind Gunnar, blocking the entrance. Those close to the scene moved away while others watched in silence. The blue parasite disconnected from his junkie puppet and scuttled away with his tentacles waving in the air. The music and auctioneers stopped with a display of death now the source of entertainment. Kora sized up her opposition and tossed back her tan ankle-length cloak to show her weapon on her hip.

The dog-faced man and his posse of three criminals howled with laughter. In an instant, Kora had her weapon in hand and dropped one of the thugs with a shot through the chest. The dog-faced man growled with the others and charged toward Kora with his gun aimed. "Kill her!"

Gunnar rushed toward him. The unexpected blow knocked the dog-faced man's weapon from his hands. He delivered an uppercut and multiple blows to Gunnar's face. Gunnar stumbled back against a table filled with drinks that tipped over and splashed everywhere. Before the dog-faced man could grab a broken bottle, Kora gave him a hard punch to the ribs and a knee to the face as he doubled over. The others rushed to attack Kora.

In an unexpected turn, shots whizzed past Gunnar and Kora. One of their attackers fell to the ground. The hooded patron at the bar had a pistol drawn. With brisk steps, he strode toward Kora to help kill the dog-faced man and one other left alive. Both tried to get their own shots from behind an overturned table, then crab-walked in opposite directions whilst shooting. Kora and the stranger pressed their backs to each other to counter the shots. The dog-faced man cried out from a shot in the shoulder. The stranger managed to hit one with shots in the belly and neck. The dog-faced man held out, ducking behind another overturned table. He stood one more time, bleeding from his mouth and shoulder. Kora dropped to one knee and shot him straight through the chest. He jerked backwards with the impact. He gurgled and spat blood into the air as he lay dying on his back. Kora rose to her feet and approached him. Without any hesitation, she unloaded her weapon into his body.

Just above the shots, one of the thugs grunted as he tried to lift himself from the ground with his weapon. Kora began to swing around, hearing one left alive. Before she could shoot, the hooded patron had shot the wounded man. Blood soaked the stone floors and thick ornate rugs.

The rest of the bar resumed their previous activities. Kora's unexpected ally removed his hood with a hand that had a ring on every finger. Each one from a different world. He was young, with glacier-blue eyes and stubble around his mouth. His greasy blond hair was pulled back. He glanced around at the carnage. "Impressive." He then began to rummage through the dead's pockets.

Kora didn't react to his flattery. "Were those Hawkshaws that paid you working for the Motherworld? I don't like bounty hunters."

He paused and searched her face while also looking at her unusual gun. "I didn't ask. And to be clear, I don't like bounty hunters either."

Kora maintained her cool, knowing he wanted to know as much about her as he could get. "So you're a gun for hire?" she asked while looking at Gunnar, who appeared in over his head as he wiped blood from his face. She motioned for him to come over.

The man scoffed as he rose to his feet. "No... That's not my thing. Just not willing to die for someone else's problems. I'm an opportunist I guess."

"A real hero, huh?"

"Look. I can get you to Pollux. You're trying to find General Titus. And I'm willing to help... for a fee."

"Uh, understand, we're just simple farmers," Gunnar said.

"We're searching for soldiers for a fight against the Motherworld. We have some money, but this is not the one you get rich on," Kora said.

The man and Kora locked eyes. He nodded his head and ran his hand over the crown of his head. "I understand. Still, pay me what it's worth to you."

Kora looked at Gunnar, who had a glimmer of hope in his eyes. "We're ready when you are."

"Come on, my ship's down at the port. My name's Kai, by the way."

Kai turned to walk out the front doors. Kora and Gunnar followed behind and into the light. All three squinted and covered their eyes after emerging from the cloistered brothel that made its business by stealing time and money. The streets were busy with people minding their own. Kora loved the small farm and its sense of community, but if she went back, it would never be the same. She would be known as a warrior again, an angry warrior exceptional with a gun and... But that couldn't be changed now. Nothing was ever the same once the Motherworld found its way into your orbit.

As they entered the hangar, Gunnar's mouth and eyes looked like yawning uraki. "What..."

Kai smiled as his head arced back. "She is a Tawau Class Freighter. Don't ask me how I got her. Setting course for Pollux. I need to stop on Neu-Wodi first. You know, there's a rancher there. He has a man that might just work out for you."

Kora glanced at Gunnar, who nodded. "Is he worth our time? Because we can't afford to waste any," asked Kora.

Kai looked up at the freighter. "I think you'll like him."

Gunnar was still taking the sight in. Kai watched him with curiosity. "You ever been off planet?"

Still taking in the size of the ship, Gunnar shook his head. "No."

"What did you do on the farm?" asked Kai.

"Oh, I oversee the harvest, and planting, and cataloguing seeds, and making sure that—"

"He's a farmer," interrupted Kora.

"That sounds great. You might want to hold on." Kai pulled back the throttle. The freighter lifted off the deck and launched upwards. *"Whoo!"*

THE MEADOW, LUSH WITH KNEE-HIGH WILDFLOWERS, WAS EVERYONE'S FAVORITE place in spring. It was a place for meditation and reflection. Many babies were conceived under the cover of a blanket of fresh blossoms. A handful of villagers, four uraki being led by the reins, Den, Hagen, Sam, and Aris strolled through the grass discussing the potential battle. Sam slowed her pace for Aris to catch up. He seemed shy around the villagers, as he still wore Imperium-issue clothing. He had to keep up appearances when they asked for transmissions.

A look of shame crossed his face when they were near, but Sam couldn't help but notice how handsome he was without the burdensome armor he wore when he first arrived. She could see who he really was, all of him without the heaviness of the Motherworld or bloodshed. Aris stood up for Jimmy and her, even when it seemed suicidal. Sam wanted to get to know him. She hoped he felt the same. He stopped and scanned the landscape with longing and sadness. She wondered what such a worldly man saw when he took in their village. He saw their world; however, he appeared to be far from it in that moment, lost deep in memory and emotion.

"It's beautiful, isn't it?"

He turned to her and smiled. "Better than an Imperium ship. The company is better, too."

Sam fiddled with her apron. "So, you've been sending messages to the Dreadnought?"

"I have. Status reports to ensure that everything's going according to plan."

Sam's face brightened. "*Our?* You with us now?"

Aris pulled out a long fuzzy weed from the ground and toyed with it. "Sometimes you have to pick a side. I suppose I am… if that's alright? Not sure what the others think. I'm not with the Imperium by choice."

Sam watched the rest of the villagers walk ahead of them in the distance. They appeared small and none of them carried weapons. Having an army or soldiers was never the village way. Their existence had been peaceful and isolated; the closest villages and towns were days away by foot. She didn't care if Aris wasn't born there or even on Veldt. She had learned the hard way that home and family sometimes came from different places.

"Can I ask why?" she asked.

He turned his head away from her to hide the lingering shame. "You don't want to know the things they made me do. You'd think differently of me."

Sam ducked slightly to catch his eye. "I do. If you'll tell

me. What you did for me already makes you different."

Aris looked into her eyes. He didn't hold back the pain or memory of his father's death still etched into his sight, a constant feature of his nightmares. He opened his mouth to speak when Den's voice bellowed across the meadow. "Here! We found it!"

Den waved his arm toward the villagers holding the reins of the uraki. They surrounded a dropship, dirty from being left out in the elements. Except for symmetrical patches of red on the front, it was nearly identical to the ones the soldiers arrived in. Thick, deep grooves behind it showed where it crashed and skidded until it stopped. "We need to get this thing out of there," Den called out.

Sam glanced at Aris in wonder after seeing the ship. Both jogged to catch up with the others. Aris moved closer and walked slowly around it to get a better look at the damage to the ship. Hagen approached him. "You really think you'll be able to get it running?"

Aris scrunched his face and watched closely as part of it moved out of the dirt when Den attached ropes from the ship to the uraki. "Let's see what we've got when they pull it out. How long did you say it's been here?"

Hagen looked into the distance. "It's how I first met Kora."

Hagen often wandered out past the village alone, because this was where he scattered a portion of the ashes of his wife and daughter. He spoke to them when he needed to.

It made him feel less alone, but also afraid. When would be his time to go? Would he spend his final day decrepit and alone, bedridden? That seemed worse than death. Since the deaths of the two people closest to him, he felt like he merely waited to go to the other side himself. What a welcome relief to see them again. Yet, he didn't have it in him to take his own life. It seemed unnatural and a dishonor to the others who were taken against their wishes. His wife had been born with a weak heart and his daughter inherited the same condition. It took them both.

Age gave him patience. And so, he waited and walked as long as his aging body would allow. He stood in the meadow with his head to the sky when he saw a meteor entering their atmosphere. But it wasn't a meteor. He could tell by the way the light reflected off the surface and what looked like smoke trailing from the back. The ship looked out of control and was heading straight toward the meadows. He watched it careen then tumble to the ground. It didn't break apart upon impact but slid across the field. Smoke rose from the crash site and some sort of alarm pinged at regular intervals. He looked toward the village, wondering if he should alert others first, in the event that whoever was inside wasn't friendly. But he didn't want to cause trouble or panic. What if someone inside needed immediate help?

He ran as best he could toward it. One of the doors was ajar enough for him to see a semi-conscious woman. Kora lay there, her eyes only thin slits, looking toward the crack of the open door and holding her belly. Hagen gripped the edge of the door with both hands and moved it to see if she was in need of immediate assistance. It was difficult at first as he strained against the weight, but slid open once he could fit half his body inside.

Her eyes shifted toward him then shut again. Moans of pain escaped from her lips as she clawed at her belly. Hagen lifted her shirt just enough to see under her hand. The area surrounding her ribs was bright red, and in a few days would be badly bruised. He wouldn't be surprised if a few were broken. She didn't make any sense when she tried to speak. He thought perhaps she also hit her head. But the pain in her eyes when her gaze met his. It was worse than anything a body could experience. He didn't have a clue what she had been through or escaped from; however, it was enough to risk her life for.

As he looked around to find anything that might tell him who she was or what had happened, a pistol lay on the floor behind her. It was beautiful in its craftsmanship. He didn't know much about weapons, only what farmers needed in the event of putting an animal down, or for hunting. Hagen didn't care for Providence much. Part of him wanted to walk away, let the gods decide. But the song his daughter used to hum popped into his head. No, he couldn't leave her like that. His Liv would not think twice about helping.

He asked, "Can you try to walk? We aren't too far, and I can get help halfway there." Tears streamed from her eyes, but not a sound from her lips. She shook her head. "I will be back," he said. Before leaving, he took the weapon and hid it in his tunic. She was probably very perceptive, but under the veil of her blinding pain, she didn't notice.

Hagen left the ship and ran back as best he could, ignoring his own pain in his joints. Sometimes life made him acutely aware of his age; sometimes he ignored the reminder. As he neared the village, he saw Gunnar inspecting the fields. He had an uraki with him. "Gunnar! Thank the gods."

Gunnar took his waterskin and offered it to an out-of-breath and red-faced Hagen, who bent over with both hands on his knees. "Everything alright?" asked Gunnar.

"There is a ship in the meadow. A woman's inside, she's hurt. Take the uraki and get her out. My home is fine. I'll go tell Sindri and meet you there."

Gunnar nodded and took hold of the uraki. Gunnar trusted Hagen and didn't ask more questions as he walked in the direction he was told. It didn't take long until he saw the ship. The sight made him move quicker. Nothing like this had ever occurred in his life, or to this village. He peered inside and saw the woman. Her eyes were shut. He rushed to her side to see if she still breathed. It was shallow, but there. She moaned slightly at the movement of him scooping her into his arms and her eyes fluttered at the pain, but there was no other way to get her to safety or see the extent of her injuries.

He sat her on the uraki and lay her torso against the back and neck of the beast. Gunnar removed his shirt and placed it beneath her face for comfort. Before leaving, he closed the door of the ship. With one arm slung over her back and the other holding the reins, Gunnar led them back to Hagen's house. He kept one eye on the path and the other on the face of this intriguing stranger.

Hagen and Sindri waited outside. When Gunnar approached and carefully took Kora off the uraki, Hagen opened the door for him. The bed was prepared; Hanna the midwife waited inside with her basket of glass bottles filled with herbal painkillers and tonics, bandages, water, and fresh clothing. She would see if there was a serious injury. Gunnar lay Kora on the bed. He didn't know why part of him ached the way he did seeing this complete stranger in this state.

Her eyes opened. "Where…?"

He held her hand. It felt cold despite her face and hair being covered in sweat. It stuck to her cheeks and forehead. "Doesn't matter now. You're safe. Rest and we will do what we can."

Kora moaned and nodded. Gunnar gave her a smile and left her with the midwife, who began to remove her top and tend to her injuries.

Once outside, Sindri had a look of concern. "Do you really want to invite this into our village?"

Hagen scowled. "What else was I to do? Leave her there? Abandon her at the gates of Providence? If my Liv hadn't succumbed to her illness, she would have been ashamed of me not offering help."

Sindri shook his head. "If she is to stay then she is your responsibility, Hagen. We don't need trouble. We aren't prepared for it. We have done well to look after Sam, but she has been one of us since birth."

Gunnar watched the two men debate before speaking up. "I will also help. She… I don't get a bad feeling from her."

Sindri glared at him. "Because she is beautiful, eh? A pretty damsel in distress."

Gunnar blushed. "It's the right thing to do."

Sindri thought for a moment giving them both hard stares. "Fine. Both of you. Until she is awake, and you know more, she stays here. I don't want her wandering the village and I get every villager pounding on my door with questions."

Gunnar and Hagen nodded and glanced at each other. Sindri glowered at them, then walked back to the longhouse. Gunnar turned to Hagen. "I will bring you extra supplies of food, lamp oil, and firewood so you don't have to wander out, and I will come by every day to check on you."

"Thank you, Gunnar. And I agree. I feel she is in need, real need, but doesn't mean any harm to us."

Gunnar looked toward Hagen's house then turned to leave with the uraki. Hagen took a deep breath and looked to the sky. "I believe I have made the right decision. She was brought here for a reason. If you can hear me, Liv. Thank you for your guidance. Watch over me."

Aris placed his hand on Hagen's shoulder. "I will do my
 absolute best."

The old man gave him a warm smile. "I trust you will, especially knowing how you tried to help Sam. That took real courage and bravery. Your father and mother raised you with honor. They would be proud."

Aris averted his eyes and looked into the distance. "Thank you. Thinking about them is not easy…" He took a deep breath. "Anyway, it's nice to be around good people again."

Den climbed out of one of the ditches behind the ship and stood before the villagers. After Sindri's death no one volunteered to lead, and no one questioned Den's unofficial appointment to the position of village leader as the villagers came to him for advice or to organize them when the village needed to gather. He was younger than any previous leaders; however, with the looming threat, he seemed like a natural choice given his physical strength and prowess as a hunter. He took the position with humility, even though he didn't hold back from delegating tasks or asserting his opinion. Den liked that he could finally have the chance to prove himself beyond his labor. "We have to work together now. Everyone take hold of the rope… Ready… heave!"

Everyone did exactly as told, including Aris. The uraki dug their hooves into the ground and pulled with loud snorts and brays. The villagers grunted and held onto the ropes, even when they slid through their fingers as they felt the weight of the ship once it was released from the compacted soil. Inch by slow inch it slid up the side of the crater. It would gain some purchase then slip again.

Being one of the largest, Den pulled at the end. "Come on! We do this together or not at all. Our lives are on the line," he shouted, encouraging them to keep the momentum despite the strain. The uraki didn't like the noise or being pulled so hard. They were used to being in the fields and pulling logs or stones, not ships, yet even they toiled and struggled forward.

After a grueling half an hour, the dropship teetered over the lip of the ditch until it was free from where it landed. The villagers released a collective sigh and cheered and embraced each other at their accomplishment. Den went to each participant to pat them on the back and make sure they were okay after the extreme exertion. Sam brought water around the group to cool them down and hydrate. Aris ran to the metal carcass to give it a quick inspection, and peeked inside through one of the windows. He pressed on the seam of the door to release it. It opened slowly with a creak. Hagen and Sam appeared next to him. With his ever-optimistic grin, Hagen slapped him on the back. "What do you think?"

Aris looked to the sun, and to the moons beginning to make their appearance. A cool breeze rustled his hair. "I think we're staying the night. We brought a few tools, not knowing what the damage would be. Might take some time, and that is if we don't need parts."

"I'll start the camp," said Sam with excitement in her voice. She looked across the meadow to the forested hills as she walked toward one of the uraki with supplies tied to its side. She thought she saw a shadow, but it must have been the shape of the trees in the waning light. Most of the villagers left after doing their part, but Aris, Den, Hagen, and Sam remained.

Well into the night, Aris fiddled with the controls with what tools he had. He pulled on a metal lever on the control panel, only for his hand to slip. A loud crack to his knuckles made him cry out. "Damn it!" He gritted his teeth and rubbed the back of his hand. Sam came running in. "What happened?"

Aris shook his head and bent over to pick up the fallen tool. "I'm not sure I can fix it. Not with these tools anyway."

Sam took the wrench from his hand. "You need rest." She led him by the hand to a seat behind the cockpit. "Wait here. I will be back."

She rushed out of the ship and returned moments later. Across her body she carried a leather satchel. Inside was a waterskin. "Here. Have some."

He looked at the waterskin then back to the uncooperating cockpit controls before taking a long gulp. The look of longing and sadness from earlier in the day crossed his face again.

"What is it?" Sam asked.

He hung his head and stared at his Imperium boots. He hated them. He'd have thrown them into the fire with the Imperium corpses, but he had nothing else to wear. They were a reminder of Noble and that day. "If I can't fix it, we won't have the guns, and I know we need them."

"Everyone sees you've tried your best. Kora will bring us men to fight. Maybe we won't need the ship's guns."

He looked into her eyes and placed his hand on hers. "No. We will need everything. I've seen what that ship and the men aboard it are capable of."

Sam's hand curled over Aris's hand. He took a deep breath. "They don't take just anyone as a soldier. Not until they're sure they've broken you. Broken everything about you. They came to my world... they made my father kneel before me and told me to kill him. They told me if I didn't... My sisters, my mother, they said they'd..."

Sam squeezed his hand.

"I'm afraid. I don't want to scare you, Sam... but I'm very afraid."

Sam wiped a tear from one of Aris's eyes. "It's alright. I don't have parents either. My father left for Providence and never came back, and my mother, not knowing what to do with her grief, told me she was going to collect firewood during one of our big snows. She walked out in the calm white and never came back. I think part of her doing that was not being able to heal herself like she could to others. When she lost the will to live, she lost something very sacred and special within her. Something I am just beginning to understand.

"I was raised by this village. Now I take care of myself, but if I should need anything I know I can count on the people here. You can count on me. And when you do return home and want some company, well, I'm not going anywhere. I've never been anywhere else." She leaned her head against his shoulder as they sat in silence for a moment.

Aris handed the waterskin back to her. "You're right. It's getting late and I won't be any good if I injure myself. I'll help finish setting up camp." Aris made makeshift beds outside of the ship for the night. He and Sam found it more comfortable to sleep beneath the stars than inside the ship in disarray. Sometimes it made him feel better, to gaze at the same stars he could see from his home planet. At other times it filled him with regret.

Despite his angst over the uncertainty they faced, he fell asleep quickly to the sound of the breeze in the trees and nocturnal birds singing their songs. For a moment he thought he could be back at home. He dreamed about his father wearing his crown and carrying his rifle as he walked through the fields with a dead animal slung over his shoulder. He didn't stop but walked toward the ship. He looked back at Aris and smiled. Aris wanted to run to him but couldn't move.

He tossed and turned until the sound of the fire and rising morning light caused him to blink his eyes. He could smell cooking but didn't know if that was a dream or real. Then a bang. That was real. He sat upright, putting his hand on his weapon. The sudden movement disturbed Sam, who wiped her eyes and looked around. Everyone was still asleep. Near the fire was a roasting alpine deer on a spit. Its antlers were removed, but not in the vicinity. Hanging from a crudely made rack of branches were about a dozen fish drying.

Sam turned to Aris with a confused expression. "Did you…"

He shook his head. "No… and look around. There is no trail of blood or sign it was prepared here. Whoever did this isn't in the camp. But I dreamed…"

"Den?" said Sam.

Aris looked in his direction. Loud snores and heavy breathing were all that came from Den. "Don't think so. His bed looks undisturbed from last night. Hagen couldn't manage all this on his own that quickly."

There was another bang and blue light coming from inside the ship. They looked at each other. Aris whispered to Sam, "Wait here."

He rose to his feet and grabbed his weapon. With slow, steady steps he approached the open entrance. The ship hummed when he entered, but no one was there. He walked into the cockpit to see the ship running diagnostics. It was repaired. A hand on his arm made him jump. "You fixed it." said Sam.

"Not me," Aris said, looking around for any evidence of who could have done this. He kneeled, seeing a few scattered tree needles and dirt. No boot prints. There was only one who came to mind. He rushed outside and looked to the hills.

Sam stayed closed. "What are you thinking?"

He continued to peer into the dark. "Jimmy… It was Jimmy. I know it."

Both squinted to see if anything, or anyone, moved above them, watching them. The morning mist had a yellowish glow with the rising sun. Shadows moved with the rocky surfaces. From a distance they could see his glowing eyes as he stood tall. Sam glanced at the food waiting for them. "I hope he comes back. He doesn't have to be alone out there."

He didn't hear Sam's screams. It was the gunfire that alerted Jimmy that something was occurring in the village. He knew Sam was on her way home alone after leaving him by the water. It was enough to get him on his feet and running toward the noise. As he got closer, he made his hearing more acute. He knew Sam was in trouble. He ran faster toward the granary where he sensed the fight.

The scene made him stop in the doorway. His mind calculated what he saw, but it was what he felt that made him take action. It was the same deep connection and feeling of loyalty to Princess Issa that made him choose those who were kind over the perpetrators of hate and war. This was a scene he had witnessed many times before, but he had his orders. His actions were not his own. And he knew how these scenarios ended. He made the choice to disobey orders and kill the soldier hurting Sam and threatening Aris.

The same spontaneous spark of decisiveness happened when news of Princess Issa reached him, and he and all those like him discarded their weapons to stop fighting. No one understood it except them. Her presence, and what she stood for, expanded their man-made consciousness to desire a deeper purpose. They could learn and feel for themselves as their consciousness evolved. That was the first time he had killed anyone in a very long time; however, there was no way he would allow anyone to hurt Sam. Deciding to defy protocol made him flee from the granary.

Sam made Jimmy feel the spirit of Princess Issa again. There was something special in her touch, healing almost. In that moment he knew he had to choose what he would be. He chose to do what was right. But it was also right for him to leave again, to be in the wilderness that called to him. He stopped running when he reached the spot on the rocks by the river where he left the flower crown Sam made for him. He picked it up and began to hike toward the forest. The deeper he ventured, the freer he felt.

He found a small clearing and decided to camp there for the time being. Although he had left the village, he would not abandon Sam or Aris. Jimmy sat down, not knowing what to do next. In the darkness, lights began to spark around him. He held out his hand to catch one. It fluttered its wings, and he knew what it was – a firefly. It was attracted to his eyes that glowed like them. He felt a glow coming from within that he could not explain. It was clear what he would do. He would be a silent watcher, only interfering when needed.

Not far from one of his legs, he spotted a long-fallen branch. He took it in his hands and ran his fingers across the wood. He looked around until he found a rock. With three hard whacks he chipped it to create a sharp enough edge to begin to carve into the branch. He didn't know what he was creating just yet, but it would pass the time. By morning he decided it would be his staff.

Enough time had passed that he wanted to check in on his friends from afar to see if he was needed. In the fields, he grabbed some cloth attached to a scarecrow. It would make the perfect cloak as he wandered in and out of the forest. He wanted to be something more than just a metal body. Jimmy watched Aris and Sam walk with the villagers and a few uraki toward the outskirts of the village. He wondered what they were up to, and decided to follow in silence. Then it came into view. An abandoned dropship. Jimmy knew the model well. If they couldn't get it running, he would do what he could under the cover of darkness. They also didn't appear to have much in the way of supplies. He had an idea and turned to venture into the forest again. Before doing so, he flipped his staff, so the pointed end was now at the top.

The darkness of the forest canopy enveloped Jimmy like a cloak. He knew there were so many creatures who thrived here. It was teeming with life. Again, he would take one of them so his friends could survive. This was part of the cycle of life. Some had to consume others to live, and it went all the way down to the tiniest bacteria in the soil beneath his feet. All living things had to be fed. Jimmy felt no remorse in hunting despite his great respect for all creatures great and small in the forest. He waited in the brush until the alpine deer came into sight. With perfect, calculated aim, he threw his staff in its direction. The animal flew a few feet then fell to the ground with a hard thud. Birds scattered from the surrounding trees. Jimmy ran to its side. After dark he would take the fresh meat for his friends to eat and check on their progress with the ship. He knew there would be items he could use living out here. He felt around for the right size rock. The forest floor was not short of them. When the right one came into sight, he felt a surge of energy, like those fireflies swirling around his eyes.

After leaving this feast for his friends, he climbed a small rocky outcropping. Both Aris and Sam looked in his direction. He turned and retreated back into the forest. He found a log to sit on and consider what the possible outcome of their endeavors would be. Not far away, on the ground, were antlers and a partial skull covered in moss. Mushrooms grew from the now decayed carcass. He ran his hand across his head. In that moment he had an epiphany. *Self-determination is what shapes the individual. And a free mind, a free soul is a great thing capable of extraordinary feats… but it is in the unswayed choice to surrender one's freedom to Issa, where our hearts are truly free, in perfect communion with her love.*

KAI SET THE FREIGHTER FOR LANDING AS THEY APPROACHED NEU-WODI. KORA took long gulps of water from a steel bottle and handed it to Gunnar. "Stay hydrated. You will need this."

Gunnar took the bottle and finished it. The doors to the freighter opened and blasted them with temperatures beyond anything Gunnar had ever experienced. The valley on Veldt had its own microclimate surrounded by mountains. There were seasons that never strayed too hot or too cold. This was infernal heat that instantly dried their sweat. The sensation of thirst hit their mouths and throats with the inhalation of brittle air that tasted like licking a hot rock. Dust kicked around them as they jumped from the loading ramp to head toward the village. Kora used her coat to protect her mouth while squinting through the intense sunlight. Gunnar pulled his shirt over his nose and mouth, and shielded his eyes. Their exposed skin warmed to the touch. Kai led the way through barren streets and closed shutters of the low adobe-and-stone village buildings and houses. Some were painted white to reflect the heat. Nothing green grew to provide shade: what life could thrive here? Their pace was slow but steady through the thick air and heat that taxed their lungs.

There were, however, large spires of hardened sand that stabbed toward the sky. The sun beat hard above their heads with a hot breeze blowing across their faces. They stopped at the entrance of an iron foundry made from stone. Kai approached the building and a sizable man in his sixties in a mesh shirt, with straggly gray hair and a mustache, greeted him. He wiped the sweat off his balding head with knotted misshapen hands and gave him a large grin of gold-plated and rotting teeth. "Well, if it isn't the bastard from Saaldorun. What brings you all the way out here?"

Kai chuckled. "I missed your smiling face, Hickman. You still got that man chained in the back?"

Hickman glanced behind his shoulder then back at the three. "Tarak? Yeah, he's working off his debt to me. Another couple dozen seasons, we should be square. What's it to you?"

"Mind if we talk to him? There could be a deal in it for ya."

Hickman nodded his head. "Well, if there's money to be made…"

The heat outside was scarcely tolerable and the ironworks even less so. The rhythmic sound of metal hitting metal filled the large workshop, crowded with all types of weapons and iron parts strewn on tables and in boxes. At the very back, by another large doorway, stood a shirtless man with shoulder-length wavy brown hair tied back. He had three lines tattooed at the base of his throat, a black square on each tricep, and a square-like key pattern on his hands. Sweat rolled down his bronzed face, neck, and torso as he hit a glowing metal rod against an anvil. His eyes remained firmly on his work.

"Hey. Hey! Tarak!" shouted Hickman.

Tarak glanced up then returned to his creation. The ringing of metal hitting metal filled the entire room.

"These people want to talk to you."

Kora approached him. A thick iron chain ran from the anvil to his ankle. "What got that chain on your leg?"

Tarak continued to hit the anvil. "A long road of mistakes. But if you're here to accuse me of crimes against the Motherworld, I'm guilty as charged. Take it up with him." Tarak lifted his ankle and flicked his head toward Hickman.

"No. That's… That's not why we're here." Gunnar said. "We're here from a small village, and we're looking to hire some fighters to train and protect us against a force from the Motherworld."

Tarak stopped hitting the metal rod and looked up at her. His previous dismissive, uninterested expression turned serious. Now he listened, but still regarded the trio with skepticism. "I'm no friend of the Realm. That's well known. And I'd gladly fight with you, but I have a debt on my name, and I honor my debts."

Kora turned her attention to Hickman. "What's he owe you?"

Hickman mumbled to himself and wiggled his misshapen, calloused fingers as if he was trying to come up with a sum. "Uh… 300,000 Darams ought to cover any inconvenience I've suffered."

"Oh, ya bollocks," cursed Kai.

Kora scoffed. "We don't have that kind of money."

"No money?" Hickman said, confused by the concept.

A loud shriek emerged from the open back entrance to the foundry. Hickman gave her a wide grin. The gold in his mouth shimmered in the light of the blazing furnace to his right. "Well, I do love to gamble."

"Ah, here we go," said Kai tiredly.

Kora turned to Tarak, who stopped his work to listen with a silent intensity. He gave her a short nod.

"What's the bet?" she said to Hickman.

His eyes moved toward the direction of the continued shrieks. Gunnar followed his gaze. When he saw the creature, his lips parted and his eyes went wide. "Holy hell. What the…" Just outside was a corral made of iron and wood. Three men tended to a magnificent creature of great stature, an oversized hybrid of bird and animal. He had an immediate tightening of fear in his belly, along with utter fascination. Part of him wanted to see it up close, and another part wanted to turn and run if they had to do anything with it. How could any human be a match for it or tame it? Its thick, muscular hind legs kicked up dirt while its clawed front legs attempted to scratch three ranch hands trying to take hold of it. Loud guttural cries escaped its black beak that could rip off the scalp of a man in one swipe. Its shiny feathers were the color of soot beneath an oily sheen. He could hear Hickman chuckle. Gunnar glanced around, hoping his face or body language didn't betray his conflicting emotions. He pulled back and crossed his arms.

"See that creature out there? It's called a Bennu." Hickman said.

Kai chimed in, "How the hell did you even get one of those? This isn't their home."

"I won the creature in a game of chance on Samandrai. After a few shots of spirits, it seemed like a good idea because their loyalty is unmatched. They will kill for you. But the damn thing won't let anyone near it. Even killed a man who tried to feed it. I said I would give it six more months then it would be slaughtered for meat and the feathers sold by the bushel."

Kai nodded. "Who am I to judge?"

"If Tarak can break that creature out there, his debts are squared with me," said Hickman, a little dejected as he stared at the creature.

"You get nothing for nothing in life. What are we putting up?" Kora asked.

"If he don't ride him, you all get a chain and shackle. That's the deal," said Hickman.

Tarak no longer looked at Hickman or Kora. His gaze was fixed on the Bennu with confidence.

"Can you ride him?" asked Kora.

Without turning back, Tarak answered, "Yeah, I can ride him." He swung his hammer in a wide arc, hitting the chain attached to the shackle on his ankle. It split in two with the softness of an overripe fruit. He looked at Hickman while kicking it off then walked out the back door toward the corral. He rolled his bare shoulders while flexing his back muscles. Without the shackles, he appeared taller and wider.

"Hehe. I have to see this," chortled Hickman as he followed behind Tarak. Kora and Gunnar joined him at the edge of the corral. Hickman nudged Kora then spit in the dirt. "Not sure about this. With his history, he runs given the chance. Let his own people die at the hands of the Realm. Some men you just can't trust."

Tarak entered the corral with the ranch hands still struggling to control the Bennu without losing their lives. It pecked its pointed beak toward them with fury in its eyes. "Drop your leads."

One of the hands shook his head toward Tarak while gritting his teeth. "She'll tear you apart."

"Drop your leads and clear out. Now."

The creature stood on its hind legs and let out a half-squawk and roar. The three ranch hands nearly toppled over one another. "Suit yourself!" shouted one of them as he let go of the leads and ran to the entrance to the corral. The other two looked back and didn't waste time sticking around. They dashed away at the same speed. The Bennu fell back to all fours as it studied Tarak. He held out a steady hand and made eye contact with the

Bennu. Its yellow eyes shimmered beneath the blazing sun. He kneeled in front of the creature and bowed his head. When it approached close enough for their heads to just touch, he spoke to the creature in his native tongue.

"Shhhh. I'm not going to hurt you. You're far from home and so am I."

The Bennu listened without attacking. "You and I, we're alike. We've been hurt, betrayed, our trust has been broken." When he stood before her, he stroked her thick feathers that turned to a softer down toward the end of her torso. The Bennu rolled her head at his touch. She stood easily quite a few feet taller than him, with broad shoulders that appeared even larger up close. Tarak rested his head against her chest and synced his breathing to hers. He closed his eyes. "We both know fear. Yet, the biggest fear we both face is the fear of ourselves. Let's show them we're not afraid. Let's show them we're more than the shackles that bind us."

"Well, I'll be…" whispered Hickman to Kora.

Kai slapped him on the arm with the back of his hand. "Looks like you might lose this game of chance."

Hickman shrugged. "Either way I win. Once it has been mounted a single time, I can do it again. And it will know it can be conquered. I'll be its master."

Without prompting, the Bennu bent its front legs and bowed its head. Tarak leaned against its ear. "Thank you. Let us show them who we really are without fear."

Confidently but with care, Tarak grabbed the rope the ranchers had left behind and lassoed the beak before moving onto the Bennu's back. He climbed on, patted its neck, and it leapt into the sky. The Bennu shrieked as it circled and dived around the corral. Tarak leaned into its neck. It flew straight for a tunnel of lethal sand spires. Tarak and the Bennu whizzed through. Its giant body soared through the air with ease, but it resisted Tarak's guidance. The Bennu bucked and bashed against stone cliffs. Tarak continued to hold on until it tossed him off onto a rocky outcropping. Tarak rolled, then jumped to his feet to run at speed to catch the creature. With perfect timing, he jumped from the outcropping back onto the Bennu's back. This time, instead of fighting, they were flying. The Bennu continued back toward the corral then dived deeply toward the onlookers. They all crouched to the ground except Kora. She looked up and smiled as the rush of wind from its flight blew her hair into her face. She raised one hand to feel its feathers.

Tarak sat upright again and the Bennu circled slowly until it landed back in the corral. He gave her one last pat before climbing off. Hickman stood and clapped. He entered the corral. "Well done!"

Tarak stood before him. "Hickman, I've done as you asked."

Hickman couldn't contain his eagerness to touch the Bennu. His eyes were fixed on her. "Your debt is square with me."

Tarak bowed his head. "Be good to her."

Hickman stepped away before Tarak could finish this

sentence. He motioned with an impatient wave for the

ranch hands to enter the corral with him. Tarak stopped before walking through the ironworks toward the freighter. Kora looked back at him watching Hickman have the ranch hands assist him mounting the Bennu. He kicked his legs into her ribs and tugged on her feathers. "You're mine now. Go." It launched into the sky with rocket speed and bucked with its full wingspan on display. The sharp motion threw an unsuspecting Hickman to the ground. "Whoa! Whoa!" he screamed as he coughed blood, lying on his back. The Bennu dived from the air and landed on his chest. Her talons embedded in the meat of Hickman and probed deeper as she pecked at his skull and face until it was a bloody pulp. Meat stretched and tore as her powerful beak consumed him. The ranch hands ran past the feasting Bennu, back into the ironworks. Tarak continued to watch the Bennu with its kill. It turned to him, giving him a knowing look, then bolted back into the sky and out of sight with Hickman's body in its talons.

"That a girl," Tarak said.

"How did you do that?"

He smirked. "They are indigenous to my world. I grew up with them my whole life and my first love traded in their feathers once they died."

She gave him a smile and led the way out toward the freighter.

Kai had already begun preparations to leave when Kora and Tarak entered the ship. "This was good. Anyone else you know of along the way?" asked Kora.

Kai gave her a cocky smile. "I might have a couple ideas."

1

CASSIUS PACED AROUND THE CONTROL DECK WITH HIS HANDS CLASPED behind his back. He awaited a call from the Motherworld from a man who made him feel more unease than Noble sometimes did, or the priests that he didn't really feel were necessary on the missions to each world. It was the reason he didn't have any of the implants the Realm's upper classes and high-ranking officials made to their bodies. This would leave him essentially open to others in ways he didn't want. Once you were plugged in, there was no way out. At some point he might do *something*, otherwise his loyalty would be questioned. He remained in his position for now because the cost of climbing up the chain of command within the Realm came with a very high price.

He waited for a call from Enoch, one of the high scribes with abilities that defied logic. Unlike the priests, his presence was scarce, albeit one that was always in the know. With Noble, Cassius knew what he could expect. There were no limits to his depravity or lack of mercy. He was an indiscriminate killer. Enoch was a man who felt like a phantom and wormed into your thoughts and brain. His power extended beyond the ability to wield a weapon or carry dusty trinkets called holy relics.

The comms blinked red. There was an incoming transmission. Enoch would not show himself, he didn't need to. His voice was enough. "Noble and Cassius. The Regent requires an update."

Cassius stood at attention out of instinct, even though he was the only one on this deck. "Admiral Noble has entrusted me with this call. He is… indisposed at the moment."

"Very well. What news?"

"We are still pursuing the criminals Devra and Darrian Bloodaxe. Anyone caught aiding them will be held accountable. But we are close. We have eyes and ears in unexpected places and Hawkshaws on their trail. You need not worry."

"Worry? We never worry. There is nothing remarkable that has ever come from Shasu. They play a game they cannot win. Just know that we too will hold anyone accountable not doing their job to their best ability. This chase stops now. It is a drain of energy on the plans we have for the Realm. When you hear from me again, I expect to hear they are dead."

The comms blinked again, and Enoch was gone. Cassius relaxed his tense body. He had to tell Noble the recent developments with the Hawkshaws, and that *they* were being watched by the Motherworld.

Cassius wasn't a war orphan or impoverished villager sucked into the Motherworld's war machine. He was the son of a family not from Moa, but which had been there for many generations. They were accepted because of their wealth and station at the time. Janus and Vesta Falto were his parents. For years, they enjoyed the riches and splendor of the Motherworld. The falcon was their sigil, and it was on everything that belonged to his family. His mother especially relished their status, always having the best of everything since birth. She adorned herself with the finest jewels found in the depths of Daggus and fabrics from far-flung worlds to show off at parties and official functions. She spoke multiple languages.

Cassius stood next to his parents at many of their functions, dressed like a miniature senator. His role was to be seen but not heard as the next generation to represent their family. He was an accessory to his parents, a model family of model citizens carrying on the glory of the Realm. He listened to adult conversation with intensity, observing everything. "He's just a child," they would say of him before continuing to discuss politics or court gossip. But beyond the veneer of success, both had addictions that sealed his fate at a young age.

Vesta had every new biological enhancement on offer. And Janus, to pay for his wife's every desire, made deals with the wrong people and created large debts. Their fights echoed through their home with Cassius lying awake in bed, listening.

She would scream that their winter home needed another renovation, the previous enhancement to her body needed to be tweaked. He returned her demands, threatening to leave her for one of his lovers who gave him what *he* needed. In the morning the calm returned, and they lived in harmonious, elite misery. The house staff never spoke of their fights and Cassius never brought it up. He remained good, doing as he was told to avoid either of their moods or demands placed upon him. This carried on until just after his fifteenth birthday, when he received his first rifle made from gold and rare petrified ebony wood from Shasu. A falcon adorned both sides of the butt of the rifle.

Senator Remus arrived late in the evening. It was an unusual time for guests. Cassius crept from his room and watched from the shadows and behind corners until Remus was in his father's office. He stood behind the door to listen to the unusual business that had to be occurring. Would his father leave again for "official business" and into the arms of the many lovers who demanded nothing of him?

"Senator Remus, to what do I owe this unexpected visit?"

"I wanted it to be unexpected. There would be no excuses to face me or the business at hand."

His father stammered. Cassius could hear the

nervousness in his father's voice. "And what business is that? I can assure you all is well in my household."

"That is not what I have heard or know. As you may or may not know, Master Information is audited. Especially of those who must be held to a different standard. Your wife's enhancements have left us privy to your personal circumstances. And I have been alerted to your mounting debts. We can't have this with a senator of your standing. The Realm doesn't tolerate men of low or common character. You are lucky your family name is one dear to the Motherworld. You must live up to it."

"I promise to pay it all back. Whatever Vesta owes, and the guarantees I have made… Give me time."

"You are out of time. Payment must be made now."

"I have nothing. It's all gone except for our homes and their contents. The minimal staff we have are paid with accommodation and food."

There was a pause. Cassius's heart pounded in his chest. This was bad. He could feel it.

"You have your name. And everything and anything in this universe can be considered currency."

He could hear his father's heavy breathing. "The boy. You can have the boy. He will serve the Motherworld well."

Cassius's heart sank as he felt his fate tossed in the air like a coin in a game of chance. His body trembled hearing how quickly his father would barter him. He had been used as a pawn in this adult game he didn't fully understand but knew he hated. His family and all their friends were frauds.

"Yes, the boy would clear everything. Tomorrow, he will be collected by a priest and taken to the monastery to be further educated. Depending on what we see in him, he may go to the military academy after."

Cassius didn't have to hear more. It was enough. He ran to his room and shut the door. He looked out the window to the three moons shining upon him. What his father did was unforgivable. It would be the last time he would ever see or speak to them.

Cassius awoke to their maid wheeling in a large breakfast with all his favorites. Crispy thinly sliced meat sat on toast dripping with melted butter. Sliced fruit, sweet cream buns, and a smoothie of wild berry yogurt was presented on a silver platter. His stomach growled. At fifteen he was always hungry. But it was a pathetic way to say sorry or goodbye. It made him feel cheap. He stood and got dressed, leaving the food.

He walked out to the main sitting room, where both his parents were drinking tea and talking in hushed tones. His mother stood first with her surgically enhanced youthful skin appearing shiny and tight. Both were dressed formally for a guest. She opened her arms. "My darling. We have the best news. You have been selected to enter service to the Imperium early. This isn't granted to many. It is an absolute honor for our family to continue to be of service to the king. You can carry on our bloodline and keep our name in its rightful place in the Motherworld."

Cassius remained stoic, ignoring his mother trying to

embrace him. He stepped back. She appeared hurt by this and dropped her arms and her smile.

"Did you hear your mother? This is great news. You will become a senator like me one day, or something greater. I know it is very soon, but you leave today. We didn't want you to miss out on this opportunity."

Cassius looked at them both, his hate and sadness battled in a duel in his soul. Both his parents were liars and cowards. "I understand," he said as he turned and walked to the entrance to wait for his fate to arrive. It didn't matter if it was five minutes or five hours. This was no longer his home. He had seen the priests, heard of their vital role in adult conversations, but they mostly creeped him out. He sat on the long bench with his hands on his knees as he stared at an oversized painting of three of them. If he could, he would take a blade to it and shred it to pieces. His father's footfalls could be heard to his right. "You didn't eat your breakfast and said nothing to us."

Cassius turned to face his father. "There is nothing to say. It has been decided."

His father opened his mouth to speak when the maid approached with a small packed bag. She placed it on the floor. "Sir, we received a transmission. The priest has arrived."

Cassius stood and grabbed his bag. His mother entered with tears in her eyes—which used to be black but were now a light shade of blue after her last round of implants. Her tears meant nothing. All their secrets and lies and memories didn't belong to them, they were part of the collective pool of information the Realm used as their own type of currency.

A loud bell made her jump. The automatic front door opened. Cassius stared at the priest, who wore heavy red robes despite the summer heat. His clammy white face with a greenish undertone wasn't masked, even though it looked like he wore one. It had the appearance of a death mask. His clasped thin hands. Red and blue veins below his skin looked like webs.

"I am here to collect what has been promised." His voice didn't match his appearance. It was deep and heavy. In the dark it might make you think you were in the presence of a ghoul.

Cassius picked up his bag. "I am ready to go."

His mother grabbed his arm with his back turned to her; however, he continued to walk out the open door and past the priest. Her fingertips slipped off him. He didn't look back, because seeing their faces might make him as sick as having to leave with this strange man of faith in red.

Cassius waited next to the transport vehicle until the priest caught up to him, walking at a slow pace. "You may enter. It is a short journey to the dropship. You will find the monastery is very different to here."

Cassius didn't respond. What could he say? He entered the vehicle, never to return.

The priest sat across from Cassius. His pale eyes and face didn't stray from him. Cassius remained silent, ignoring the mounting tension, the unsaid expectations from this moment forward. The priest was the first to speak. "Being silent is a valued trait in the priesthood. Observation will give you a power those who prefer to hear themselves speak do not have. Do you agree?"

Cassius shrugged. "Just don't have much to say."

"Mmm. I doubt that. Well, at the monastery you will find out if this is your path."

"What if I don't want to be a priest? My father wanted me to be a senator."

"Your father has no say in the matter. You belong to the Motherworld and live exclusively for its glory. We will observe you and decide."

They arrived at the monastery three days later in the middle of the night. There were very few lights to be seen on the approach. His time here would be spent in remote isolation. The castle-turned-monastery was on a world swallowed by the Motherworld in one of its many campaigns. The grand building, made from white and gray basalt columns, sat high on a plateau that overlooked a vast sea. The forest that once flourished around the castle had been burnt to the roots in the final battle and never grew back. The castle had belonged to the once-king, who died the day the Imperium arrived. Because of the library that possessed fifty thousand books from across the universe, the priests petitioned to take control of it. It was graciously given to them.

Cassius walked through the main corridor with strange objects beneath spotlights in wide alcoves. He stopped in front of a large scepter made of bone. The priest stood next to him. "See, you are curious. This is the Golden Scepter. Over there is the Book of Law, with the monarch's bloodline, and there are so many others."

Cassius remained silent, but this did not enrage the priest. He turned on his heels and began to walk again. The sound of their footfalls was the only sound in the dimly lit building until they reached the end of the hallway. Cassius didn't see another priest. They took a right down another corridor with several steel doors placed at regular intervals. They stopped in the middle. "Here is where you will stay. A seminarian will be here in the morning to go through your schedule. In one year, it will be decided if you remain or go to the military academy."

"I have no say in the matter?"

The priest looked into his eyes as if he could read his mind or see into his soul. It made Cassius want to run. He was here because someone got into his mother's brain and knew all their secrets. "Do any of us have any say in our fate or the struggles we encounter?"

The priest pressed a single glowing red button in the center of the door. It opened. Cassius looked inside. It was sterile and spartan.

"Sleep well, Cassius."

"Thank you." Cassius entered the room and shut the door with the controls on the wall inside. He placed his bag on the floor and sat on the bed. He didn't believe any of what these priests or the Motherworld preached. But there was no escaping any of it. He'd find a way to live, then maybe a way out would present itself. The universe was a big place.

He owned a villa on the Motherworld dedicated to pleasure and a little pain, but when not there (which was often) he had other means of release. Noble moaned as the slick black tendrils kneaded and probed his body. The tightening of their grip around his cock, wrists, and neck made him forget who he was and that anything existed outside this bed chamber. He liked to feel his windpipe constrict until the lack of oxygen gave him a sense of lightheaded euphoria. Miniscule suction cups invisible to the human eye titillated him to a pleasure most humans didn't know existed. The Twins had come to him as a gift from a warlord in a world rich in phosphorous. It was the only present he ever received in his life that meant anything or gave him real pleasure. Few things satisfied him.

He arched his back and tightened his ass as he cried out in ecstasy. His eyes bulged and the cords of his neck felt as if they would snap as he was taken to the edge of death, seeing the birth of stars every time he found himself in the grip of the Twins. They released him when he orgasmed for them. His bodily fluids lapped up right after. Their slimy tentacles loosened, and he blinked his eyes before stumbling back. "Let me watch you now."

He lay on a chaise and took a hit from a hookah next to him filled with poison leaf and spice berry. He pressed the wide mouthpiece into one of the many thin red patches of skin on his torso that would mainline the poison leaf into his body. The room filled with the Twins' gurgling and hissing on his bed. Two knocks broke his viewing of the Twins writhing in inhuman shapes.

"Come in."

The door slid open. Cassius peeked his head through the opening. He glanced toward the bed then snapped his eyes toward a nude Noble, who lay with one leg on the ground and the other outstretched. His flaccid cock was in full view, with a string of semen webbed onto his thigh. "Cassius, please join us. Would you like to go a round with the twins? There's no better exercise than wrestling on these long voyages." Noble wiped the white liquid from his cock with his finger and flicked it toward the bed. The Twins gurgled and jumped as it landed on them. Noble chuckled. "The Twins are insatiable. I'd love to know who created them."

Careful to hide his disgust, Cassius pursed his lips, keeping his eyes on Noble's face. "Thank you, sir, that is tempting, but I have other pressing matters. We've received a communique from the Hawkshaws. They're requesting to rendezvous with us. They've captured a creature that has information about Bloodaxe and her brother."

Noble's eyes narrowed with another hit from the hookah. "You are dutiful, aren't you, Cassius? That's excellent. Inform me when they arrive." He exhaled a cloud of smoke in Cassius's direction, sending the sweet scent of poison leaf. "And the transmission from Enoch. Did he seem satisfied with our progress?"

"He seemed so. They want this wrapped up sooner rather than later."

"I do not cut corners with my missions. But all this is excellent news. Come back when the Hawkshaws arrive."

"Yes, sir."

Noble rose to his feet, dropping the hookah, and took languid steps toward the Twins. Cassius watched Noble gaze down at the beasts changing color and size. Noble threw his head back with his mouth and eyes opened wide as the Twins gripped him again. Cassius snapped his head away, not wanting to know this much intimate information about his superior. Cassius saluted and shuddered as he backed out of the door that automatically closed and locked behind him. He paused for a moment and heard, "Again. This time I'll go deeper, and you go harder."

Cassius walked down the corridor, remembering those first days of meeting Noble and how he became his first-in-command.

The monastery and priesthood didn't work out for Cassius. The priests loathed his irreverence and sent him packing to the military academy after he received notice his parents were stripped of everything that once made their family great. He refused to eat or leave his room in the monastery. Cassius felt destined to spend his life in the military, because he had no fortune and a family that couldn't help him in any way.

Atticus Noble walked through the corridors and into the training pits with a confidence that Cassius didn't possess. Atticus had no problem making his opinion known or asserting his will upon others despite their protestations. He won most people over with his charm because even though the Noble family was from Moa, it was unremarkable in wealth or status. When Cassius stood alone at the far end of the mess hall, Noble strode over to him. "I wondered if you would be here."

Cassius gave him a confused look then glanced at the two other recruits standing in silence behind him. "How do you know who I am?" asked Cassius.

Noble smirked. "It is known in certain circles what happened to your family. No hard feelings, I hope. *My* father was only doing what was right."

Cassius didn't need to know more. Aristocratic families on Moa and senators clawed for power and favor no matter the cost, especially those at the bottom. "I haven't been in my family home for some time. Now I never will return," said Cassius.

Noble placed a hand on his shoulder and smiled. "I know that too. You cannot be held responsible for the sins of the father. Perhaps one day you can regain the dignity for your name. Stick with me. Maybe I can help."

Cassius nodded. He wondered how much Noble knew of his parents' fall from good standing and into the ultimate shame of having nothing. The gall to begin their conversation like this shocked him. He shook off his anger, only out of necessity. Here and now, he had to focus on getting through training. There was nowhere else to go. Noble was an enigma, but Cassius had learned the only way to be certain of anyone was to observe from a distance. He wouldn't make the same mistakes as his parents. "Thank you. I appreciate the goodwill."

Noble walked away with the two others in tow and his head held high as others greeted him as he passed. Cassius claimed his simple, bland meal and sat alone. It wasn't until a few months later that Cassius saw a glimpse of the real Noble, the ruthless and cruel side.

Atticus pressed the recruit's face into the slit-open animal carcass. The stench of piss and the burst bowels of the creature filled the air. Some recruits gasped, others sniggered at the sight. Noble's eyes were wild as he gritted his teeth. He didn't just try to defeat his opponents, he needed to humiliate them. Cassius stood next to Noble, watching the scene without commenting or showing emotion.

"You see, Cassius, Braun made us lose the simulation today. Worse than that, he refused to admit to it. This is how we should be teaching those to aspire to be the best, for the glory of the Motherworld, of course."

Vomit dribbled out of Braun's mouth as Noble kept his knee on his back and his arm twisted painfully out of the socket. "I am sorry! I was wrong!"

"Hmmm. It's too late now, but you should also apologize to Cassius. He tried to tell you and you didn't listen. Your arrogance made us fail!"

"I am sorry, Cassius. You were right."

Cassius remained silent, not needing an apology. He had simply told Braun he was wrong in his direction of the simulation. Noble said nothing during their disagreement. It had been his way to surround himself with a few individuals who were slightly smarter, yet lacking his determination or ambition. Eventually, Noble wormed his way into the right circles, rubbing shoulders with the right people.

Noble stood and wiped his feet on the grass. He glanced around at the gathering recruits, who didn't say a word. "I think we have made our point here, Cassius. Let's go."

Cassius looked down at Braun, who had his head hung low. He stepped over the carcass and followed Noble back to the training facility. He caught up with Noble. "Was that necessary?"

Noble stopped and looked him in the eye. "I thought you would be more grateful, but I understand. Your father obviously didn't know how to guide you, or himself, for that matter. He would be alive if he did. So I will forgive that question this once. You see, Cassius, it was necessary because we have to be the ones who *do*. Who else will do what is necessary when the time arises? That is what will set us apart from all these other rats."

Cassius gave him a short nod. He wouldn't argue because no one else had ever done something like that for him. Certainly not his dead father, who found himself executed by, perhaps not better men, but certainly men who knew how to get what they wanted. Like Noble and

his father.

. . .

They left Neu Wodi, the sparse, scorching landscape of sand and rock pockmarked from ancient asteroid impacts, for Daggus, a crowded city planet with every species practically living on top of each other like the plastered posters and graffiti on any available space along the miles and miles of alleys connecting the buildings. The cobalt mines put this world on the universal map and brought every species across the universe here to hack through the mantle of the planet. No space was left to be considered sacred for the original inhabitants. Forests were cut back to make way for quarries. Rivers and lakes dammed for the fresh water to be used by processing companies. When all the aquatic life was gone from overfishing and pollution, large cesspools of waste replaced them. Huge blocks of housing and infrastructure for the workforce and shipment companies leveled the surface. Indigenous life died out, leaving very little of what Daggus looked like before the mining took over. Black smoke billowed as high as the skyscrapers. Some of the buildings were new, with bright lights and constructed from the newest tech. Others were left unfinished by developers that ran out of money midway. They stood like the cement-and-metal corpses of a bloated industry. Then there were the buildings that were sad remnants of first habitation, that were now for the poorest of the poor and squatters. All they provided was protection from the elements. Still, many remained and died there with little else to hope for.

Ships of all sizes and makes whizzed past each other in flight, cutting through thick smog that never fully cleared for long. Kai took the small band to a cheap noodle shop. Gunnar stood in front, not knowing where to look with the multitude of sounds, languages, and lights stimulating his senses from all directions. The largest town he had been to in his life was Providence.

"Who are we asking to join us today?" Kora asked Kai.

Kai motioned for Kora to take a seat at the bar. "A killer. A ruthless killer. Given your skills with a weapon, you two should get along."

Inside, a creature with an elongated face and even longer jowls stood chopping slimy purple tentacles before placing them in bowls. The backsplash in the kitchen was thick with hardened yellow grease and blue flames leapt high on the outside of a pan. The restaurant was simple in design with only one chef, who seemed immune to the heat and popping oil. Patrons waited patiently for their food on a long L-shaped counter. There were few items on the menu, so the small crew readily ate what was served before them. Gunnar took a few bites from the greasy bowl with some sort of small shellfish stuck to the bottom and sides. He pushed it away and took a gulp of his beer. Tarak had finished shoveling his portion and stared at Gunnar's.

"You gonna finish that?" His voice took Gunnar away from his beer.

"No, no, go ahead," said Gunnar.

Tarak licked his lips. "You sure? I'd never steal a man's woman or meal."

Gunnar slid the bowl in front of Tarak. "Enjoy. I'm more of a slab of meat guy."

Kora paced in front of the row of seats at the bar. She didn't hide her impatience. "How long are we going to wait?"

Kai looked up from his bowl and wiped his lips smeared with chili sauce and grease. "I mean, we aren't robots. We got to eat. Relax, I put out the word. Give her a chance, she'll come."

Kora turned to him. "We're wasting our time just sitting here. Every moment that passes is a moment we're not mounting a defense."

Steam from the kitchen cleared. A woman in loose black clothing held a teacup in hands that appeared gloved in metal. Her face was hidden beneath a wide-brimmed hat. "You're looking for me?" she asked, devoid of intonation or emotion as she looked up.

Kai glanced back at Kora then to the woman. "That depends, are you the one they call Nemesis?"

She scanned the bar and lifted her head to lock eyes with Kora. "I am. Why do you seek me?"

Kai grinned and crossed his arms, glancing back at Kora again. "See. Told you I'd find her. Might be about time you lot start trusting me."

Kora stepped toward her, "We need people like yourself." Before she could continue, shouts and screams outside the noodle shop caused Nemesis to turn in her seat. People called her name throughout the streets. But it didn't sound like a party. A woman wailed amongst the shouts. A man nearly passed her before stopping and doubling back. He appeared to have come from the mines. The skin beneath his eyes hung low and dark. His clothing tattered and dirty from a day's work.

"Nemesis! Nemesis! Please, a child was taken…"

"Is it…?"

He nodded his head while looking at the band of strangers who didn't appear like Daggus working folk. "It's Harmada. She's—she's acting insane. She killed a security guard; we have her cornered in the bowels but she's threatening the child and we just…"

Nemesis turned to the warriors who sought her. "We move. Then we can see if we can work together."

Nemesis rose from her seat. She had two swords holstered on either hip that were as eye-catching as her two hands. Kai, Kora, Tarak, and Gunnar followed Nemesis and the man through the alley outside the restaurant, until they reached an open metal elevator overlooking the cramped city. The melting sun on the horizon set the smog alight. The man smacked the button with a glowing arrow. It brought the elevator alive with a jolt moving toward the bowels. The deeper they went, the hotter and damper it became. The dim light showed very little except more graffiti and condensation.

"So, what's the job?" Nemesis asked Kai.

"We represent a village on a small moon called Veldt. This village faces the threat of annihilation by the armies of the Motherworld. With your reputation, we thought it might be something you'd be interested in.

"And you want…"

Kai took a deep breath. "We are looking for warriors to join the fight and protect them."

"You're taking this handful against officers and soldiers of the Realm?"

The elevator came to a sudden stop. "This way!" said the man as he rushed forward.

Kora caught up to Nemesis before she was too far away or headed into a nasty fight. "We are. We will try." Nemesis gave her a nod before moving toward the group of people talking amongst themselves. One of them stood hunched over, sobbing. They were tenants in the bowels and those from above who knew the missing child. No one moved past where the overhead lighting stopped and instead hovered around the mouth of a maze of alleys that twisted like the pipes above their heads. Steam and heat escaped through the walls and ceiling.

Nemesis walked in pace with the warrior group. "This sounds like a suicide mission to me."

Gunnar looked to Kora then Nemesis. "We think we stand a chance. It's all we have in this universe. We have to try or die trying."

"I respect that. I'll join you if I have the chance to spill the blood of officers of the Realm," said Nemesis as she scanned the dark alleys ahead.

"You'll have that chance," said Kora.

Nemesis touched the handle of one of her swords with a light sound of metal on metal. "We will talk after this."

Kora moved her coat away from her hip before Nemesis could walk toward the unseen menace. "In case you need it, I have backup."

Nemesis studied Kora's pistol. "Let me handle this. Harmada has grown accustomed to the pain of her grief. I know her rage intimately. We are not enemies."

Kora nodded and made her way to Kai to tell him to hold any fire too. A woman who had exhaustion etched in her face and deep creases for a woman twice her age ran up to the two female warriors. Her eyes were bloodshot from crying and her voice was hoarse. "Nemesis! I beg you! I have nothing to offer, but please! She has my daughter."

Nemesis looked over the crowd, who had all eyes on her. Loud enough for the group to hear, she addressed them. "Hold her."

Two women linked their arms with the sobbing mother and gave her a look of pity. Nemesis broke through the onlookers and into a darkened alley. There was no telling how far it went, as the floor and ceiling disappeared in the pitch-black darkness. The floor and walls about ten feet ahead glistened with a thin slime. Condensation dripped with cables hanging from above. They appeared like a circular web. A perfect hiding place. The hum from the city on top of them seemed to send a vibration through the walls. The scent of urine and excrement from the homeless wafted in the heavy air. Unpleasant, but not unfamiliar to Nemesis. She stopped and lifted one arm to her side, gripping her sword with her other hand. "Show yourself. We know you are here. I just want to talk. That's all."

Not a soul made a sound as they waited for Harmada to show herself. Everyone knew crowded, dark spaces could be dangerous. Individuals went missing all the time in Daggus without any care or concern. But the children in DCB (Daggus City Block) 410 went missing at an unusually high rate. The problem with Daggus was the extortionate cost of living, leases arranged by employers were on a ten-year basis. Leaving early meant hefty fines that low-paid workers could not afford, and there was always someone to take the housing, or the job.

No one left, they couldn't. Working on Daggus began with many promises, but always ended in poverty. The exploitative contracts left little room to move, and anyway, where would they move to? Back to their home planets destroyed by the Realm? Dead worlds that had left desperate refugees.

It was this need for a home that had led to the settling of Daggus. The first mining company, Tecton Cobalt, created locally, eventually merged with and received help from a larger corporation that footed the bill for all the major infrastructure to the virgin planet. With the cost so high, greater margins meant more for the company and less for the workers. This laid the foundation and precedent for how business was done. It was a place where great fortunes were made, and many lives lost.

The bowels of DCB 410 were littered with bloodied shoes, toys, clothing; however, no one could figure out who would commit such heinous crimes against the innocent. The cops were not paid enough to risk their lives. They did the basics to keep business running smoothly, domestic issues didn't matter to them. Dead kids didn't matter.

Sometimes vigilantes went down to patrol. They never came back. The bodies were never found, and therefore the Daggus Council refused to spend the money to send regular army patrols. The company that owned the building said it took no responsibility according to Section 7.1 of the leases. It was the responsibility of the parents to keep their children safe. After fundraising and local shop owners chipping in their own money, the residents got permission to put up cameras. It took only two weeks for the culprit to be caught. A half-blind retired mole miner pushing a hundred and ten years old, living on floor 400, was the one to recognize the half woman/half spider with the body of a child wrapped in white webbing. He told them through weepy, pale eyes, "They called her Harmada… a species from the indigenous culture here."

The residents tried to close off the bowels but were blocked by the company owners. It breached health and safety. Their only hope was Nemesis. Her meeting with Harmada was long overdue and that moment had arrived. Nemesis had attempted to corner Harmada before, to speak to her; however, the indigenous creature knew every corner and alley better than anyone. She was there when it was all built. She had escaped one too many times. The creature had to be exhausted from this constant chase.

Nemesis removed her hat and gave it to the man who had summoned her. She had a black silk scarf tied around her head to keep her hair out of her face. A series of pops and cracks, like branches being stepped on, emanated from the darkened center of the cables above. Six hairy needle-like legs descended from above their heads. A bulbous, oblong body topped with a woman's pale bare torso and bald head striped with blue emerged from the darkness. In her arms she dangled a small child no more than ten years of age. The young girl sobbed, her entire body trembling from fear. The spider woman glared at them with ten obsidian-black and red eyes they could see their reflection in. Nemesis took her hands off her sword and lifted them above her head.

"Stay back!" the spider woman hissed.

"I just want to talk. That's all," Nemesis said.

Harmada bared her spiked teeth. "I'm clearly desperate, that's true, but I'm not stupid. I know why you're here. You've come for this child."

Nemesis remained calm. "Yes I do."

A long hiss escaped Harmada's lips. "You can't have this one. This one is mine."

"She has a mother who's waiting for her. Who's missing her."

Harmada opened her mouth wide. Saliva dripped from her teeth onto her flexing bony right hand. "Is that so? And I'm supposed to care about that mother's pain? Who's here for my pain? Look at this place. This was my home before they came. My home for a thousand generations. Taste this air. It's poisoned my children. My eggs have become so fragile in this toxic air. My children are too weak to emerge. What about my pain? I want justice." Only hate, the kind of rage that builds from the darkest of caverns of a dead soul, reflected in her eyes. All ten eyes magnified the grief that had hardened to grotesque blood lust and fury.

Nemesis continued to listen. "I understand, but this is not the way. There is a difference between justice and revenge."

"Is there? I'm not so sure."

"I know a mother's pain. I know the loneliness of that pain. But you can't hurt that child. I won't let you."

Harmada squeezed the child's leg, digging her nails into her flesh as she shrieked with wrath. Her voice bounced against the walls with the child's cries of pain. "I believe you. But understand. I will kill this child and I will keep killing until every mother weeps tears of regret for ever having come to the mines of Daggus."

One of Harmada's stinging, sharp-tipped legs stabbed toward Nemesis. The warrior swordswoman lunged out of the way to avoid being skewered, but her left arm was grazed. Harmada's leg had ripped through cloth and flesh. In an instant, Nemesis drew her swords, raised them to protect herself from a still-stabbing Harmada. The furious creature shrieked before swiping again. The tip of a leg went straight through one of Nemesis's gloves. The energy within crackled. This time Nemesis did not hold back.

Her swords became imbued with the power of the ancient blood and wisdom of her ancestors. And that blood took the form of molten lava heat that dwelled within the swords. They glowed brighter like seething rage as the heat radiated from the center and spread across every inch of metal. The brightness of the fires of Byeol could be seen as they were prepared to strike a foe. She placed both in front of her and drew an incandescent circle around her with the heated tips of the swords. When Harmada struck again, Nemesis was ready and sliced the air with her left sword. One of Harmada's legs flew into the air, releasing squirts of viscous greenish blood. She cried out in agony and dropped the child.

Until now the band of warriors watched from behind Nemesis, allowing her to take the lead, knowing she didn't want to kill if she didn't have to.

When the young girl hit the ground, Gunnar rushed toward her as she held her leg in pain. Harmada inched toward them despite her wound still gushing a viscous goo. The stink of decay filled the tight space. As she lifted another leg to stab the crying child, Gunnar snatched her away. The back of his jacket received the blow. Harmada didn't miss a beat and jutted another powerful leg toward Gunnar. With only inches to spare, Nemesis's sword caught the razor tip of Harmada's leg before it could stab straight through Gunnar's right eye. The screech of metal and bone reverberated throughout that sector of the bowels. Nemesis swung one sword around to catch Harmada's legs, but the spider scuttled up the wall in a flash. With hands splayed, teeth bared, and legs poised to stab, she dropped from the ceiling onto Nemesis. The warrior was pinned to the floor. Saliva dripped from Harmada's mouth. Her wet-tipped stinger swayed near Nemesis's throat. "Many have tried, and many have failed. I have killed more of you and I'm still here."

Nemesis grunted as she brought her legs toward her chest to kick the stinger away. Harmada bucked from the blow, giving Nemesis a chance to sever another leg, unleashing more putrid goo across the ground. Incandescent with fury, Harmada attacked Nemesis with her remaining strength. Nemesis matched her movements in a sword fight between steel and barbed bone.

Their cries and grunts rang through the alley until Nemesis twirled with balletic precision on her knees. Her crisscrossed arms swiped across Harmada's belly before she jumped to her feet and brought her swords down on Harmada's neck like an executioner. Harmada's body collapsed in a twitching heap. Small shriveled, unhatched eggs spilled from her gut in a thick black clotted mucous along with a web of hardened gray tumors. The stench overwhelmed the warriors and onlookers, who covered their faces. Then hundreds of spiders scurried across the ground and into the bowels of Daggus.

Nemesis bowed her head and put her swords away. "Find peace," she said to the dead spider woman. The band of warriors moved toward her. Gunnar rose from his protective crouched position on the ground with the child, who had her face buried in his neck and arms wrapped tightly around him.

"Let me have her!" the child's mother shouted as she ran from the crowd with outstretched arms. Gunnar gently handed her back. As he looked away, he caught Kora's gaze. She smiled at him.

Tarak inspected the spider's corpse and glanced at Nemesis. "My god. Well done, that was amazing." He tried to reach out and touch her hand.

She pulled away before he had the chance to do so. "Do not celebrate this. There's no honor in this."

Tarak's cheeks flushed. "I didn't mean…"

"This could easily be any of you lying here in the gutter of some forgotten world, in the name of revenge. You would do well to remember that." Nemesis turned her attention back to Kora. She nodded to Kora, then Kai, before walking through the crowd that was taking pictures of the dead Harmada. Kai stayed next to Kora as they made their way back to the freighter, now with Nemesis on board. "What is your next move if Titus is a no go?"

She gave him a side glance. "Haven't thought that far ahead."

"Alright then, don't forget I'm on your side." He didn't seem satisfied with that answer. She watched him walk ahead of her with brisk steps. As much as she should be happy to have another recruit, they still needed Titus, as Kai had just reminded her. And up until now, none of the individuals they had encountered were connected to the Motherworld. She wondered how it would be with someone who had also been part of their war machine.

. . .

On the main deck, Nemesis focused on tending to the hand Harmada had damaged in the fight. Gunnar sat in the cargo hold alone. It was full of crates, and odds and ends and things probably not procured legitimately. He was staring at the wall when Kora wandered in. She sat next to him and gave him the same smile tinged with softness as earlier in the day. She remembered how he had protected the child with his body, weaponless, on Daggus without any thought to his own safety. He wasn't a seasoned warrior; however, he possessed the bravery of one

Kora looked into his eyes, unsure of her emotions. "That was good of you earlier. With the child."

Gunnar shied away from her gaze and stared at his feet. "I was just trying to help."

"Yes, but it's not natural for some."

He shook his head, holding back a smile and trying not to meet her eyes. "It is for you. Back home, you saved Sam without hesitation."

Kora leaned closer to him. Her face dropped and her eyes seemed intensely focused on nothing as she averted her gaze. "Kindness is a virtue worth dying for. I believe that. I didn't always. I told you how I fought on countless worlds. Well, word of my victories reached my adopted father… and the king. For my loyalty and service, I was promoted to the Elite Guard of the Royal Family. The appointment was engineered by my father. I couldn't have known it was something more. I was given the honor of being the bodyguard to Princess Issa."

Gunnar reached for her hand. She acquiesced to the

attempt at connection. His skin on hers felt good, right. It gave her courage. She gave his hand a slight squeeze as she closed her eyes. She inhaled deeply, then exhaled as if her words needed more air to get them out of her. Telling her story was a struggle. And it hurt. Gunnar pulled back his hand with a gentle tug. "Tell me. I want to know."

"Issa was a brightening lantern, a star that could be seen and felt. A manifestation of creation with the gift to ignite the very essence of the first sparks of life. This lived within her since the day she was born. The princess was named Issa after an ancient Queen Issa, the life giver. In the old stories of the queen, it was said she had the power to give life. It seemed a metaphor, or a myth created in response to the generations of war and conquest. Yet the stories still captured the imagination of the people, and it was believed that the Princess, my Princess, might have that same power. However, for others and the Jimmies, this was very real. She possessed the power to bring things back to life. It was a myth that gave hope, like a ray of light through a tumultuous storm. The story continued that Princess Issa had this gift too. Entire armies of machine warriors dropped their weapons and abandoned their posts, refusing to fight."

Kora watched the young girl play in the snow in the vast gardens of the winter castle. Not far away there was a frozen lake with brightly colored giant fish and creatures that swam just beneath the ice in a spectacular show. Pristine snow fell with a gentle caress to the face. This new position as bodyguard to the princess was as far from a battlefield as she could get. It was a welcome relief. Now she served to preserve life instead of taking it. Issa's cheeks and nose were a bloom of rose pink. Cloud-diffused light from the sun danced in her eyes. Lola, her vigilant protector, bounded alongside her with the same enthusiasm. She threw a ball hard across the garden. The forest canine galloped toward the brush where it landed. Birds burst into flight from being disturbed as the canine growled and thrashed its head, hidden in the leaves. When it returned, it held a lifeless bird in its mouth. She placed it at the princess's feet. Issa kneeled. Her bright eyes welled with tears. She slid her hand over the bird before Kora could scoop up and dispose of the dead animal. A bright light radiated from the center of Issa's palms. Kora shielded her eyes until the light subsided. Issa remained still, but the bird twitched and ruffled its feathers. Kora gasped while Issa giggled at the fluttering bird. It jumped to its feet and perched on Issa's lap before flying away.

Kora kneeled next to Issa with a look of disbelief on her face. "How…?"

Issa smiled at her. "I don't know. It sometimes just feels right."

"It's beautiful, like you. Please be careful who you show that to because not everyone will understand."

"I know. There is a maid who delivered me and still works in the castle. She said when I was born my mother nearly died. All the machines and doctors tried their best.

It wasn't until they thought all hope was lost they put me back into her arms. I didn't cry. But by some miracle, my mother healed the longer she cradled me. Everyone who was there was sworn to secrecy by my mother and father. They said I held hope like a chalice."

Kora smiled. "That is beautiful. Thank you for sharing with me. I promise to keep it a secret always."

The little girl nodded and bounced to her feet, seeing her protector with the ball in its mouth ready to play again. Kora could see a shadow in her periphery. Someone in the window of the conservatory watched them, seeming to walk away when Kora noticed their presence. Kora didn't have a clear view, but she suspected it was the king himself.

Later that night, after Issa's bedtime, the king waited outside her bedroom.

"Arthelais."

She turned sharply toward the voice, drawing her weapon. Her eyes had the coldness of the ice forming on the window. They softened when she recognized who called her name. He looked at her weapon then back at her. "Now I know you are the right person for the job."

Kora bowed her head with her cheeks turning pink in embarrassment. "I'm sorry, my king."

"No. That is why you are by her side. Assume anyone at any time can be a threat."

She nodded.

"Walk with me?" he asked.

"Of course, I am in your service." They walked through the grand hallway lined with windows and columns that extended the length of the wall.

"And how was my magical daughter today? She seemed very tired after an exciting play in the snow."

Kora smiled but paused, unsure if she should mention the bird. "She is a very special girl."

Kora didn't think it appropriate to stare at the king, but she could see him in Issa. She carried herself with the same regal confidence. His eyes twinkled with the mention of her. "Yes, she is. Most people who meet her feel this immediately. I'm glad it's you that has been charged with protecting her. She likes you, she told me. She said you weren't like those grumpy bodyguards she's had in the past. That you smile from time to time."

"My apologies if I've become too familiar, my Lord, but Issa is a special girl. It's hard to keep the proper professional distance when she shows me such kindness."

"Arthelais, please, you don't have to apologize. I'm glad you are friends. I believe she will bring a kindness, a compassion that I've lost with all these hard years of war. When she becomes queen, it will be the dawn of something better, and I think your friendship makes her safer. There are many who won't welcome a kinder Realm."

He paused. "What of your home? Balisarius speaks so highly of you. It must have been difficult to leave."

"I have nothing but gratitude for his generosity."

"Yes, he said you were abandoned by your family. So very sad."

Kora held back her confusion at this statement. She didn't want to question the king. When they reached Kora's room, she bowed. "Goodnight."

The king smiled and gave her a nod. "Goodnight and thank *you*."

Telling the story, Kora's eyes could not hide the unexpressed sorrow from all those years ago. Gunnar touched her hand. "There is more to you than you let on… to anyone."

"For years I believed in nothing until her. Then I truly had faith she could save us."

"Maybe it's the faith we feel that will save us. I have faith in you."

Kora turned to Gunnar. "We should get some rest. I have a feeling getting General Titus on board might be a little work. It can't all be this easy."

When they rose from the crate, Kai stood in the doorway. "Hey, you two. Thought I might find you in a different… position."

Gunnar stammered, with his cheeks slightly flushed. "Just talking. That's all."

Kai glanced from one to the other. "Anything I need to know as your captain?"

Kora shook her head. "You know as much as we do." She walked past Kai and Gunnar followed.

Kai stood in the doorway and scanned the hold before leaving and shutting the automatic door.

. . .

The freighter needed refueling when they landed on Pollux, home for gladiators from across the known universe. The planet Castor shined brightly on the rocky, dusty terrain despite it being dusk. Looming above them was the ancient stone Colosseum, where they hoped to find an amicable General Titus. The original town sprouted from the entrance of the Colosseum and grew like roots to the bottom of the rugged outcrop. The entire economy was built on its legacy and reputation. Generations of families called this home.

The band of warriors left the freighter for the Colosseum with Kai leading the way. Gunnar's lips parted in awe the closer they were to the entrance. Kai hit his arm with the back of his hand as they walked along the ancient hand-carved stone ramp, bleached by the harsh light. "The twin moons of Castor and Pollux are known throughout the galaxy for producing great spectacles of combat. Only the greatest warriors appear in this coliseum."

Gunnar's head arched back once inside. The phenomenal view of blue to violet bleeding to sherbet orange as they walked below stone flying buttresses was a breathtaking sight. They all slowed their pace. As they rounded a bend, they stopped to watch a monstrously sized gladiator with spiked skin and teeth fight his way to glory. He roared in victory with his large hands beating the air. The crowd cheered with him. Gladiators in leather collars of all genders, sizes, species and from all corners of the universe milled around the corridors. Blood painted the ground where bodies were dragged from the fights. Tarak smiled in amusement and pointed to one of the gladiators wrestling. "That man there. That must be Titus… General!"

A gladiator with a face that wore many wins and losses turned to Tarak. "It's not. General Titus does not fight anymore."

Tarak frowned. "But he is here! Did he lose? Injured?"

The gladiator looked him in the eyes and crossed his oversized arms, large from years of training. "Not in the coliseum. He has only one war. It's within himself. You'll find him by the Southern Gate."

He turned to a hairless servant girl with white blush, wearing rough cotton trousers and tunic. Her bright face and luminescent skin didn't need hair. She stood against the wall with the obedience of a statue.

"You, servant girl! Take them to the general."

She gave them all a placid smile. "Please follow me." They continued to follow her along the outer passage overlooking the town below until they reached an arched doorway. She released a heavy sigh and pointed. "The great General Titus."

A man still physically in fighting shape, but past his prime, lay flat on his back, barefoot, wearing nothing but a tattered, urine-soaked loincloth. His body was crosshatched with thick scars and a few burns. They told his stories in the arena. His graying beard appeared matted and unattended to. Covered in dirt, he mumbled to himself in a drunken stupor, oblivious to their presence. A large, mangey rat crawled across his belly. Tarak scrunched his face then raised his eyebrows. "Well, I hope he fights better than he smells."

Gunnar turned with a concerned look toward Kora. "Are you sure this is a good idea?"

Kora nodded. "Let's clean him up and get him sober."

Gunnar glanced at Tarak, who shrugged. "Yeah, that'll do it. I'll take this end." Tarak grabbed his hands and Gunnar his feet.

Sasha pointed toward a wash station. "Over there."

The two men carried him quickly into the round room and propped him up on a bench. Sasha moved toward the spout to release gushing ice-cold water. Titus's head lolled as he mumbled various curses and threw limp punches, splashing water in all directions. Sasha ignored him without appearing worried, probably having done this many times before to many gladiators. She grabbed a thick-bristled brush and began to scrub his body. Titus shook his head and wiped his eyes that burned through the warriors with fury, especially Kora. "Get off me! Get off! What do you think you're doing?" he shouted.

Kora stepped closer and into a puddle at his feet. "What does it look like?"

Titus remained defiant. "Go to hell. I was fine."

"No, you are not fine. Did you command the Eastern ranks for the old king? Are you not General Titus, defender of the innocent and oppressed? A legend."

Titus averted his eyes as Sasha finished her work.

"I don't know what you're running your mouth about. Why can't you just leave me alone?"

Kora matched his defiance. "Because my best hope is that long-ago general is still in front of me."

The shouts of the gladiators and clinking of metal sounded distant, almost a whisper in the room. Water dripped in rhythmic drops. Titus shook his head and his hand curled to a fist. "What the hell do you want from me?! My men are dead. I've grown tired of reliving that every day. In the coliseum my rage made me a god, but it's all used up. This bottle is my only true comfort from that hell. Now leave me and let me die in peace!"

Kora stepped closer. "I don't think you're meant to die here, General."

Titus didn't respond. He studied each of the warriors in turn. A torrent of raw emotions punched him into a moment of sobriety. "Stop calling me that. I have no rank, no privilege."

Kora kept her stern demeanor. "I'm here to make you an offer. To give you a chance at redemption."

His anger softened. "I am beyond redemption."

"I have no time for pity! What about all the dead men you once commanded? What about them? If not redemption, what about revenge?

Titus glanced at the warriors again, and their weapons. Their faces remained hard, but a tiny lightbulb seemed to turn on in the general's head. "Revenge? That might be something I can take a chance on."

Kora smiled and stepped out of his way. "Good. Take

us to your room so you can get ready to depart straight away. Need a hand?"

He stood up straight and lifted his chin. His first steps were shaky, but he continued with confidence. Titus walked slowly into the main passageway of the Colosseum. Passing gladiators stopped in shock to watch him go by with the warriors trailing behind him. He kept his eyes on the path ahead, ignoring everyone else.

His room was small with only the basics to live and sleep. There was very little in the way of wealth despite his many victories. Hanging on a wooden frame was his tarnished armor, battle-worn and uncared for. A manica in need of cleaning hung from the center, and looked untouched for who knew how long. His boots were dirty and in need of polishing. On a small table was an Imperium-issued engraved flask and his weapon.

He stopped in front of the armor, running his fingers across the embossed insignia that he had taken a blade to some time back. When he took it off in that moment, his entire being filled with shame with the memory of Sarawu.

His soldiers were dead, but he remained alive. He took a large swig of strong alcohol and stabbed through the remnants of his past, part of him that he hated and wanted to forget. His blade didn't stop until his rage subsided with each drink. That moment of despair never left. Maybe this was his fresh start, or the path to death. He touched his beard. "Give me a few minutes. It has been some time since I have worn this."

Kora touched his shoulder. "Do what you have to do."

. . .

Titus emerged from his room fully dressed and his beard trimmed to a small tuft of hair on his chin. He seemed ready to take on a new opponent. Putting on the armor had acted as medicine for the man. His eyes appeared less bloodshot and jaundiced, and he seemed to be swaying less. They walked through the village back to the freighter. "I don't think I will miss this place much," Titus said, glancing around with a small satchel in his hand.

THE HAWKSHAWS STOOD EITHER SIDE OF THEIR PRISONER, WHO WENT BY THE
name Ximon. He stood reclined in a restraint reminiscent
of a scorpion. Six metal ribs across the body connected by
a spine, with another bar that emerged from between his
legs. Overhead, a restraint jutted in an arc and held his
head in a tight crown. There was no escaping, despite his
bulk. Four robotic legs on the bottom of the seat walked
him at the same pace as the Hawkshaws. Since they'd
caught him, Ximon had cursed the moment he decided
to go to that Pleasure Emporium in Providence. Now
he was being taken to Atticus Noble so the Hawkshaws
could claim their reward. The Realm always paid well
and on time.

Atticus emerged from double doors in his perfectly
presented white shirt and black tie with Cassius next
to him. One of the Hawkshaws bowed his head. "I am
Simeon. This is the man of interest to you."

Noble looked toward Ximon. "This is the man who knows where the insurgents are?"

"It is, sir," said Simeon.

Noble walked past the Hawkshaws to face Ximon. He studied the captive, trying to judge if he was a reliable source or not. Men without any means to escape always had information that was supposedly useful. "Well, I'm listening."

"You'll let me go if I tell you what I know?"

Noble clasped his leather-gloved hands. "I'll set you free, you have my word."

Ximon closed his eyes for a moment and opened them again. He exhaled a deep breath. "I haven't seen Devra Bloodaxe for a full season, but at the time they were on Sharaan, under the protection of a king called Levitica."

"Go on."

"This was some time ago, but they were definitely there. Talk to him… to Levitica," Ximon said.

Noble smiled at Ximon and cocked his head to one side. "I certainly will. Thank you."

Noble swiveled his head toward one of the Hawkshaws, who held a gun-like tool in his hand. He opened his palm and gestured for the Hawkshaw to hand it to him. The bounty hunter obeyed and gave it to Noble. He felt the weight of the object as he walked to the opposite side of Ximon. The tool had a trigger and a wide barrel. Inside the barrel was a coupling ring and another smaller pointed barrel. Noble aimed it toward the ground and pulled the trigger. The inner barrel shot out and retracted in a hard thrust.

"What the hell!" shouted Ximon, hearing the object used. He squirmed against his restraints to see what was happening behind him. "Thought we had a deal!"

Noble stepped closer to Ximon. With the gun near the seat, the coupling rings on both glowed. "Yes... you are free."

"Well open this damn thing! I want out." Ximon's voice gained volume and panic the longer he remained in the metal restraint.

Noble ignored his demand as he matched the gun and coupling ring on the restraint. He pulled the trigger. Ximon went silent after a loud crack, followed by his body jerking once. The metal ribs and head restraints unlocked and released his body, which tumbled to the floor like a rag. His eyes remained wide open. Noble looked at him, devoid of emotion, then turned to Cassius. "Dissect his brain, see if there is anything more, then let's pay our respects to King Levitica. Hmm." He glanced at the tool in his hand. "I like this. It's efficient." He tossed it next to Ximon's body and walked away.

Cassius looked at the paralyzed man on the ground. He abhorred fiddling in brains, memories, and information. He only wanted to deal with what he could see and feel for himself. What was in front of him in the material realm. And he knew one day it might be him on the slab with his brain under scrutiny if he didn't play his cards right. But the High Scribes had founded an entire practice on it. He walked over to the restraining chair and typed on the screen on the arm. It extended from a chair to a bed and the ribs folded to the sides. Extra legs to accommodate the extra length popped out from the bottom. He looked at the Hawkshaws. "Get him back on that thing then you can go. Payment will be made when you are back on your ship. Be on standby, though. I may further require your services."

The larger Hawkshaw stopped lifting Ximon's limp body. "What's the pay? I don't sit around for free."

Cassius gave him a sharp look. "You will get paid as per usual. Unless you want to be the one plugged in then incinerated, you will be at my disposal."

The Hawkshaw growled before lifting Ximon and doing as he was told. Cassius turned to take him into the medical bay with the bed following behind. The room was fitted for the worst injuries, but also extraction. It lit when he entered, as did the hologram that automatically read Ximon's vitals. From the shadows a scribe technician emerged. "What do you wish?" they said.

"I want a full extraction, starting now," said Cassius. He turned to watch the bed position itself in the center of the room. From the ceiling, robotic arms with different medical tools unfurled. One had a laser that set a red dot in the center of Ximon's head. It glowed brighter until smoke rose from his skin. Cassius couldn't help but watch with vacant eyes as the scene made him remember what he tried so very hard to forget. The currency the Motherworld valued was blood and information.

. . .

Devra and Darrian Bloodaxe and Milius took counsel with King Levitica and General Ion in Levitica's transport vehicle, which was the same size as a dropship. The Bloodaxes shared similar features, matching war paint that extended from their brows to their scalps, long hair in thick dreadlocks and braids. Milius, a young fighter with hair close to the scalp and black grease smeared across their eyes like a mask, stood behind the Bloodaxes. Like most kings, Levitica dressed the part. His heavy blue robes that dusted the ground appeared to be mountains of fabric. His skin was the color of deep ocean pearls, with a dewy iridescence, and he had a beard of tentacles. On the top of his head were two large pink orbs for eyes and a crown made from a single solid piece of coral. It was the rarest find on their planet, and therefore forbidden to pluck from the depths of the ocean caves. This crown had been made by the first kings of Shaaran.

They drank sea grass tea for its restorative properties. Each battle wore their bodies down a little more and now they had to decide how to respond to an unexpected transmission. It was odd to hear from a woman they never heard of before and a man they purchased grain from. He was a farmer and didn't hide the fact. It didn't feel like a trap; however, the circle of those they could trust grew smaller by the day. If they knew they were on Shaaran, who else did? As always, King Levitica allowed the Bloodaxes to decide for themselves the course of action they would take. He merely wanted to help and further their cause, not dictate the direction.

"Can this woman be trusted?" Devra's leg bounced as she pondered the request by King Levitica to meet with a woman named Kora and a small group that accompanied her. Kora's message was short and to the point.

We seek to parley with the Bloodaxes. We need help.

Darrian sat next to Milius, cleaning their weapons. "She had enough information to find us here. If she was with the Imperium, there would have been an all-out attack. That is their way."

"They are in a cargo freighter and not a warship, if that helps. From our scans of the ship, there don't seem to be any large weapons on board. There are also no other ships in the vicinity," said General Ion.

Darrian looked up from his weapon. "Never underestimate how Motherworld deceives. Our struggle for freedom taught me that. Those closest can be the ones they use as traitors. But I don't think that of this Kora."

Devra touched her brother's shoulder. "I know the wound is still fresh. You're right, we must be careful. We do not know who this woman is or her intentions. Why does she need our help?"

"Being careful and toeing the line sometimes costs more than the lives in the present, or inconveniences. Sometimes radical change, open rebellion, is the only option to course correct. We are setting the path for future generations. The choices we make could be the blessings for them or the curses, the shit they have to figure out how to clean up," Milius added.

Devra listened but looked suspicious. "I wish I could

take council with our ancestors: where Father didn't get it right on Shasu, we will. We have to try. But my loyalty is to Shasu, our people, not to someone I do not know."

"You are all very different and that is why you are strong together. You each bring a different wisdom. That is why I have supported you. This campaign of creating an Imperium on this notion of homogeneous purity is vile. They respect nor value anything that doesn't serve them even at the expense of lives," King Levitica said.

Darrian stood. "What do you say, sister? I would like us to agree on this one."

She looked at Milius and King Levitica. "I say we meet her. But I want to watch them first. Tell them to wait. You learn a lot about someone with patience or lack of."

King Levitica bowed his head. "Leave it to me. I shall go and tell them. When you are satisfied, you can either meet them or send one of my guards to tell me you are not interested. I would suggest you prepare yourself for a quick escape if you feel threatened at all. I will have my army on alert."

Devra touched the king's hand. "Thank you, for everything. This is greater than just Shasu, I feel, and that is why the Imperium wants our heads so bad."

"I will leave you now." King Levitica turned to meet Kora and the other warriors in one of the plazas.

The stone city in Shaaran was part of an ancient indigenous civilization. There were parts of the city with remnants of the first temples and villages that pre-dated their written records. The city's respect for its past belied its current modernity. It had become a spiritual center in the galaxy. King Levitica had ruled for longer than he had liked, but the question of succession and how Shaaran would navigate their relationship with the Motherworld was a cause for concern amongst his people.

The band of warriors had set up a small camp next to the freighter. They were surrounded by floating pillars. Kora left them to meet King Levitica. He stood in the center of a plaza in a quiet part of the city, with two members of his court and guards

"Your patience is appreciated, and I can assure you Devra is aware of your presence. A decision when to receive you is imminent."

Kora bowed her head. "Thank you, Levitica, honored king. We await their arrival." Even though Hagen was far from royalty, Levitica reminded her of him. He gave her the same feeling of comfort and kindness. And if he helped enemies of the Realm, he couldn't be so bad. She returned to the freighter to wait with the warriors, who sat talking amongst themselves. Gunnar perked up with expectation when Kora sat down.

"What did he say? Did they tell them it was me?"

She stared at the crackling charred logs of the fire breaking into pieces. "Have patience... We tell them what we need to."

Tarak nudged her. "You see that... Up there?" He pointed toward a particularly bright light in the darkened sky.

"Yeah, I know it. The Samardrai system."

Titus looked up from the beaten-up flask he was swirling. "You know the night sky."

"Some of it." Gunnar was the only one who knew her real identity. Kora trusted these men to fight by her side, but not with that information. Not yet.

Tarak continued to look at the bright dot with a dreamy look in his eyes and a smile. "Have you seen Samandrai? It is beautiful. The original planet of my ancestors."

Kora bent her neck back and watched it blink in the far distance. "Why have you not returned if you have a home to go to?"

Tarak dropped his head and looked at the dirt between his feet. "If only there was a home standing. My people either died fighting or were enslaved to serve the Motherworld." His eyes lifted and fixed on the leaping flames of the fire. Memory and despair lived in that fire that still burned within him.

"How did you survive? You would have been a prime candidate for them to make you one of them," asked Kora.

Tarak shook his head and opened his mouth to speak but no words formed. Nemesis spoke up. "It is very clear. They died or were enslaved." Her words cut with the precision of her swords through an enemy's neck. Tarak didn't respond. His sullen expression said it all. He shot an icy gaze at Nemesis, who effortlessly matched his stare.

With her elbows on her knees and head lifted, Kora studied Tarak's face. "You left before either could happen to you."

Tarak couldn't look at any of them. Kai stood leaning against the freighter with a blade of hemp root between his teeth. He stared at Tarak. "Great, now we've added a coward to the army, that'll be a help."

Titus watched Tarak. "At least he dares to stand and fight with us now, pilot."

"I've never been a coward," Nemesis said.

"I have," Titus replied, looking down and avoiding eye contact. "War does things to people. You can never tell how they will change after it. But maybe anyone can find redemption. Maybe not, maybe revenge is the best we've got, but it's something." His eyes flicked toward Kora. "Otherwise, what else do we have? What's the point?"

Kai rolled his eyes and continued to chew on his hemp root. "Says the drunk who can't hold his piss or pay his debts."

Titus jumped to his feet and squared his shoulders as he moved to fight. Both his hands curled to fists. Kora and Tarak stood and moved between Kai and Titus. Kora stared down Kai. "Why now? What's got into you?"

"Guys!" shouted Gunnar. "Maybe now is not the time. Look." He stood and pointed to the sky.

A dozen small ships approached the plaza. The warriors forgot the squabble and turned their attention to the landing ships. They all clutched their weapons a little tighter as the wind picked up in the plaza and the ships sped closer. One of the larger ships touched down first. The belly opened with a ramp hitting the ground. Kora was the first to walk toward the ship. The rest followed.

Side by side, a man and a woman emerged. They walked with confidence. Both were heavily armed and covered head to toe in battle gear. Their combined presence and energy commanded attention. King Levitica left his entourage waiting at the edge of the plaza to join them.

Devra locked eyes with Kora and stopped when they were face to face. "I had to be certain this wasn't a trap. There are large bounties for my brother and I. Our heads would be trophies that would make a bounty hunter rich beyond his wildest dreams."

Darrian looked at the band of warriors. "Farmer, why would you contact us from this unknown and flagless vessel?"

Gunnar stepped forward. "I was assuming we had a level of trust after our last meeting."

Devra had no warmth in her tone. "We bought your grain to feed our fighters."

Darrian had the same guarded demeanor. "Do not confuse your business of commerce with our business of revolution."

"I understand," Gunnar said.

Devra nodded. "Your coming here is a great risk to us all and to our benefactor. But we are no longer in need of your grain. King Levitica's kindness has been more than enough to sustain us, so I suggest you leave immediately."

Kora stepped forward. There was anger in her eyes. "We're not here to sell grain. Gunnar's village was visited by a Dreadnought that threatens its very existence. I have recruited these warriors and given my word to bring them back and defend the farmers. But we're running out of time."

Both Devra and Darrian stared hard at the warriors standing behind Kora. Darrian furrowed his brow and scoffed, "What? This handful, against a Dreadnought?"

"That's why we have come. You have men and ships. With you we could mount a real defense."

The siblings stood in silence and glanced at each other.

Gunnar spoke up, feeling the tension. "And, of course, we can pay you with the surplus from our harvest. That's all we've got."

Devra shook her head. "My forces against *The King's Gaze*? That's suicide. That ship cannot be destroyed by a few dozen fighters. That ship and the men aboard it are world destroyers. I'm sorry, it's impossible."

Kora nodded and made eye contact with both siblings. She raised her voice, not caring if they didn't like her exasperation. "This man is not a revolutionary, he's a simple farmer. But commerce or not, his people toiled with their bare hands to grow the grain that fed you. All of you! And because of that transaction, their village is now threatened by Admiral Noble, in pursuit of your revolution."

Darrian walked toward Gunnar and met his gaze with the intensity of an exploding star. Neither man flinched or said a word. No one in the crowd breathed. Darrian stepped back to where his sister stood. "I see. I will go."

Devra's head snapped toward her brother in disbelief at his words. She turned back to Kora. "Excuse us." She motioned for Darrian to follow her toward their ship and out of earshot of the hopeful warriors. "Our victories, what few there have been, have been tactical ones. We cannot fight in the open against *The King's Gaze*."

"If the farmer found us, it won't be long before Noble does. And I will not allow another world to fall in our name."

"We attack our targets and hide from retaliation, that is how we've stayed alive."

Darrian shook his head and looked intently into Devra's eyes. "People need a rebellion they can see. A revolution they can feel. I won't hide any longer. I cannot allow another world to fall in our name. Another world where we could have done something."

Devra continued to lock eyes with him. They were hard from war and pain, yet full of passion to persevere. There was hope. She lifted her open hand in front of his chest. He gave her a nod and clasped her hand.

"And what of those you command?" She cocked her head toward the ship, where all eyes were on them.

"Their lives are theirs."

Devra looked at her brother solemnly, unsure what to say.

Darrian turned toward his fighters. His voice carried like a true leader. "These people, they've come to us with nowhere else to turn. They come seeking our help to stand against a Dreadnought of the Motherworld. Is that not what we stand for? Are they not who we once were?"

"What army?" one of the fighters called out.

Kora stepped forward. "What you see here."

"We do have farmers," Titus chimed in with a raised finger.

Darrian turned back to his fighters. "I did not say the task would be a simple one. It never is, to defend the defenseless. But is that not what we stand for? Are they not who we once were? If we will not stand with these defiant farmers to protect their home then the revolution is meaningless. Under free will, who among you is willing to die for what we believe rather than hide behind it?"

No one spoke. The tension could be felt in the atmosphere and seen on everyone's faces. Milius stepped forward and gave Darrian a sly grin.

"Milius. Why am I not surprised?"

Milius slapped Darrian on the shoulder. "I have seen you in battle. Who is going to make sure you'll return in one piece if not me? And after what happened to my world, how can I say no?"

Darrian's hearty laugh filled the cavernous space. Milius looked over their shoulder to the others, who looked at each other. Slowly, six pilots and five other fighters joined Milius and Darrian. He turned to his sister. "They have volunteered under free will."

She nodded. "I won't stop you if this is the direction you want to take."

"The pilots with leave from Blue Squadron and the fighters will be on the ground with me."

Devra wrapped her arms around her brother and squeezed hard. He held her tightly. "Thank Levitica and leave this planet. Until we meet again. Strong body."

Devra released him from the final embrace. "Stronger mind, my brother."

Darrian turned to King Levitica. "Thank you for your generosity. Should you ever need us, you know we will do our best to help."

The king pressed his palms together as if he was about to pray. "I have so very much respect for what you are doing. The blood of your mother's people is very strong in you. They are great fighters and an enemy of Balisarius is a friend of mine. As you know, the spiritual roots of Shaaran reach the soils of Shasu. Shasu should remain Shasu at its core. I believe all the worlds should retain their sense of civilization beyond the control of the Motherworld or Balisarius's nefarious plans."

"We hope to return one day." Darrian bowed his head to the king then joined Kora and her warriors. He stopped and glanced over his shoulder. "You are this revolution's heart. Beat loudly!"

The united warriors from Kora's camp and the Bloodaxe crew faced each other and made short introductions. Kai began to enter the freighter. He watched Devra in the distance then shifted his gaze to Darrian. "Alright everyone, we can have a party later. We need to move."

The warriors piled into the freighter, not knowing what came next besides bloodshed. The atmosphere had a palatable sense of momentum. Bloodaxe and his crew had been on their own since the beginning and the warriors were solo until now. They were now united against a common enemy that had been deemed by many too great to fight; however, here these rebels from different corners of the universe found themselves ready to take the fight to the Realm. Each one had their own axe to grind, but they all wanted the same thing.

Kai watched Darrian's pilots follow above them as he stared vacantly out a large window with his arms crossed. The silver rings on his hand glinted in the low floor lights below the bay window. He chewed on the skin around one of his thumbs. Kora stopped and approached him. Something seemed to be bothering him and his taunts earlier were out of order. "What's going on with you?"

Kai didn't turn to look at her. "A lot. This is a crazy fucking idea. And aren't you the least bit curious about Darrian fucking Bloodaxe being aboard? Why would he agree to help you?"

"You think he shouldn't?"

"It just seems short-sighted. I mean, he weakens what little of, whatever word you wanna use for it, there is— resistance, insurgency. For what, Kora? The chance to get obliterated by a Dreadnought?"

"If you think this is suicide, then why are you here? Probably not worth it to even be associated with us."

"I've got nowhere better to be. He does. We're facing a Dreadnought. His life and the lives of his fighters could be lost in an instant."

"It's not always rational. Sometimes it's emotional. Guilt, it's a powerful thing."

Kai broke his gaze from the window to face Kora. "Is that what you want motivating your handful of helpers? Guilt?"

She shrugged. "It's not the guilt that matters. It's where it stems from."

He scoffed and looked out the window again. "Guilt is the underbelly of honor. I think I might've had that once. Honor. Would you believe that? It's true."

Kora studied his face and narrowed her eyes. She moved so he would have to face her, and she could see him in what little illumination lit the window. He puzzled her, going from hot to cold and distant. "What are you trying to say?"

Kai uncrossed his arms and smacked a hand against the wall next to the window.

"I mean, what do you figure? I got ten, fifteen more seasons at most, before I steal from the wrong man, get stabbed to death by some dog-headed son of a bitch in a bar fight." He looked into Kora's eyes. "It's really your fault, anyway. Makin' me wanna be an honorable man. If you had more resisting power to speak of, you wouldn't need me to join you so badly."

Kora arched an eyebrow. "You're willing to fight with us?"

He grinned. "Since you're beggin'."

Kora turned to walk away. "Kai, we're not."

Kai touched her arm. "Well, since you're asking, then. If you'll allow me."

Kora remained expressionless. "Wow."

"There is one complication. The shite in the cargo hold, I got buyers waiting in Gondival. Aren't the kinds known for their patience. Might be wise to sever my ties to life as a thief before we go picking a fight with a Dreadnought. Besides, you said yourself you need me…"

Kora gave him a side glance as she moved to return to find Gunnar. "I did not say that."

"I think you did. I'll set the course and let 'em know we're on our way. Oh, shit, does that make me one of the good guys?" he shouted behind her.

Kora wandered the freighter and found Gunnar in the dining cabin. "Looks like Kai wants to join."

"Really?"

"You don't trust him?"

He shook his head. "He's a dick."

Kora leaned against a counter with the basics of a kitchen. "True, but we need all the help we can get."

KING LEVITICA WATCHED DEVRA LEAVE SHORTLY AFTER HER BROTHER. HE MADE sure she had all the supplies she could carry; it might be too dangerous to stop anytime soon. They might never see each other again. He admired the Bloodaxes for their will for a better way of life. For Levitica, it did not matter if they gave him anything in return. Good will and altruism were their own gifts. His planet, Mireea, had found peace through diplomacy and its strong spiritual beliefs, kept alive in its monasteries. It reflected their desire for all to live in a state of harmony, or at least the best they could. The Realm would always be a threat as long as it perpetuated war. Peace was something you had to fight for. His general, Ion, stood next to him, waiting to have his undivided attention.

"My Lord, are you prepared for the worst? We have spotted a large vessel approaching."

Levitica looked to his general. "I knew the risk when I set out to help a revolution. We are prepared. But do you think we will be found out? So far, we have gone undetected by those brutes. We have given them what they wanted in the past and I should hope it will allow us some grace. They can't burn every city and world. What would be left to rule?"

"I believe we are the right side of the universe. However, the Motherworld has their own ideas," said Ion.

"Prepare the army and alert the citizens. I will stay here for any visitors. If you need me, I will be in my travel chamber in meditation."

Ion bowed and rushed to begin his own preparations for a possible battle.

Levitica's eyes remained closed, and he focused on the silence. The calm before a possible storm. He hoped for the best for Shaaran and their way of life. His mind focused to avoid panic and fear. The Motherworld and the men who carried out her will wielded fear like a sword. Sometimes they didn't destroy their perceived enemy, but they made enough cuts and amputations to create fear in others. The Motherworld could take his life, but he would not allow them to destroy his peace. He would state his case and let fate decide. And that was when General Ion burst through his chamber.

"My Lord, Admiral Atticus Noble has arrived."

King Levitica rose to his feet and smoothed his robes. He had to get the Imperium Admiral out of Shaaran without any fighting. The only realistic preparation for a fight against the Realm was to avoid the fight. He marched to his fate. "How do they seem?"

General Ion gripped his weapon on his hip. "There are so many of them. Our airspace… I don't think they came here to talk."

King Levitica walked past his general and out of the chamber. He stopped upon seeing the Imperium out in full force. "Pray for us," he whispered to General Ion.

Noble stood in the center of the plaza with his ship behind him. "King Levitica. I was told you were in meditation. That is good. I hope you thought on your crimes."

"I'd like to talk."

Noble didn't respond. Instead, he had a series of cannon fire strike Shaaran to speak for him. The impact caused the Shaaran army to rush to their stations only to be met with Imperium solders cutting them down from above and from the ground. A large *pop* struck next to Levitica, who ducked instinctively. He looked to his left to see a hole through General Ion's chest as he fell to the ground. A soldier with his face covered with battle gear stood behind Noble's left side with his weapon raised.

King Levitica straightened his posture again. "Perhaps we could speak first before you destroy the rest of the planet?"

Noble raised his bone scepter and held the joint in his hand. "Tell me of the traitors of the Imperium who have made you a traitor to us. Do not think you can lie."

"The gods will judge this," said Levitica solemnly.

Noble smacked him across the face with the scepter. "We are your gods! You have no others above us!" he screamed with a flare of animosity blazing in his eyes like the reflection of the burning city behind the king.

"Devra and Darrian landed here but left straight away. That is not a crime deserving of this bombardment. We are impartial when someone is in need of help. Please stop."

Noble smacked him again across the face, harder than before, causing him to fall to his knees. He could feel his crown slipping from his head. The ringing in his skull from the blow drowned out the continued shelling of Shaaran, for a moment. The screams from its citizens remained loud.

"Where were they going next?" demanded Noble.

"I do not know. I did not ask. It is no concern of mine where they went after here. On the memory of the gods and my ancestors, I do not know." On his knees, King Levitica looked to the sky through one eye, because the other had swollen shut. If he survived it would never open again. Dropships cut through the black smoke that shielded the rising sun. He shifted his gaze around him and saw, as far as the eye could see, death. His soldiers lay dead in the pink foamy pools of their blood. Tentacles and other limbs covered the ground. The city and people he cherished were gone. Buildings, homes, and the Great Water Temple of Shaaran that once stood high in the distance could not be seen. It lay in complete ruin.

Destruction was the point. Not bargaining, negotiating, torture, subterfuge. These were tools of the less powerful. Noble had come to raze Shaaran to the ground and then ask questions. And now he stood before Levitica, straightening his leather gloves and surveying the destruction.

"I won't ask you again. Do you choose to lose another eye?"

Levitica shook his head. One of the tentacles, hanging by a few strands of purple sinew, broke off and writhed at Noble's feet. He kicked it away with a look of disgust.

"Please! I've told you the truth. I have nothing more. I have told you everything. The truth. I am begging you to spare the rest of my people. I am prepared to die for what our civilization believes. Take me."

"If only you had that faith in the Realm. Right, the truth… that you took them in… known enemies of the Motherworld. You mended their wounds, you repaired their damaged ships, all out of your moral code of honor and charity."

Levitica shook his head. "My civilization has lived and thrived for ten thousand years with honor and charity as its most valued tenets."

Noble took his scepter and placed it beneath King Levitica's chin, lifting it toward the sky. The Dreadnought loomed overhead with the heaviness of a steel crown.

"Honor, I understand. That ship is named to honor our slain father. It's called *The King's Gaze*. But charity I don't understand. Our king showed charity to an off-worlder like yourself, and in return was slaughtered for his charity. And so, we named the ship to remind us of the power in that benevolent gaze that was lost to charity, and so we would always remember that if, by God's will that gaze could fall upon us and be held for even the briefest of moments, it could change your life forever."

"You twist the truth for your own nefarious will. Goodness will return to the universe. Endless war and needless death will end in the universe. There will be one to bring it back."

Noble's face remained hard. "Today his gaze falls on you." He removed the scepter from King Levitica's face and raised it overhead, but paused. The half-blind king remained defiant with dignity and held his stare until a loud whistling broke through the atmosphere. A light as bright as a white, frozen comet blazing to the ground illuminated the sky and dropped, creating a mask across Noble's sharp features. He looked like a skull in a uniform when he swung the scepter across Levitica's face.

The ground rumbled upon the impact and a blast of heat hit their bodies. Noble turned and walked toward his dropship. More streamers of heat blasted through the black smoke and struck the planet. Cassius emerged from the dropship and ran down the ramp to greet Noble. "We have information that the Hawkshaws have found the Bloodaxes and are about to spring a trap."

Noble continued to walk up the ramp with Cassius by his side. "Some long overdue good news."

Cassius looked over Noble's shoulder at King Levitica not moving from the ground. One of the priests plucked a tooth from the king's mouth and placed it with the others surrounding the portrait of Issa. "I suppose we didn't have to stop here after all," said Cassius.

"Yes, we did, and in a moment you will see why, Cassius. I want to enjoy this." He turned at the top of the ramp and held onto the strut as the dropship began to lift off. Levitica remained on his knees, becoming smaller and smaller as the city burned and their defenses were rendered useless. More than destroyed, any trace of civilization had been erased. The planet reduced to its pre-historic state.

When they were at a safe distance, another ball of white fire hit the plaza in the exact spot where Levitica remained. "Well, prepare my gunship, I'll go ahead and personally retrieve the treasonous dogs myself." Noble stepped back and allowed the ramp to close. He took a deep satisfied breath and smiled at Cassius with contentment.

"And what orders for *The King's Gaze*, sir?" asked Cassius.

"Well, once you've razed the planet, we'll rendezvous, extract the exact location of the rest of the insurgents, and destroy them once and for all."

"Yes, sir," said Cassius.

Gondival was not known for beauty. The sky was a blanket of thick thunderclouds that dropped buckets of water onto the planet, keeping the seas churning in constant motion. As you moved eastward, lightning could always be seen striking in vicious bright bolts. Five small moons were visible when the fog and mist cleared from the sky. The largest one hung above tumultuous waters like a frozen tear. It was home to a docking point.

The freighter and six of Bloodaxe's ships glided toward

the blinking carbide docks jutting from the surface of the moon. They floated with engines spinning in unison to keep them as still as possible when the winds kicked up. Each massive plate connected to another with carbide gangplanks. Two other freighters were parked with dockworkers attending to their maintenance and unloading goods. Crates of all sizes were stacked for delivery and pick-up. There were also floating buoys and mega-cranes surrounding various stations. The haze of night with the florescent lights made the atmosphere appear bluish gray.

Kai docked at the first station he saw, while Bloodaxe set his ships on the second dock and lashed them together. Darrian and his fighters surveyed the docks after disembarking from their ships. Milius moved next to their leader. "What you thinking? I know that face."

Darrian spoke lower than usual. "Keep an eye from above. Ears open. Spread the word. This place is so open. Feel a bit naked." Milius gave him a nod and moved toward the others.

From the freighter, Kai exited first as the ramp hit the dock. He marched toward a dockworker wearing a jumpsuit. Kai spoke to the worker and pointed to the freighter as the cargo bay doors opened automatically. Kora stood at the top end of the ramp, surveying the scene. She looked down from a dizzying height at the dark waters below the docks battering spiked erosion-worn rocks. It had a hypnotic movement and sound. The wind picked up. She tugged on her cloak to bring it tighter around her chest. The misty rain settled on her skin and hair. There were worse places on her many missions, but she didn't like it here and wanted to leave as soon as possible.

"Hey, watch your step." Kora looked toward Kai. "Let's get this stuff off my ship so we can get the hell out of this wet and dreary place. The silver ones first."

She glanced at the dockworkers who stood in the distance and stared at her. She shouted toward Kai, "I'll grab the others."

The warriors were already making their way off the freighter and unloading the cargo bay. Tarak walked next to Kora, carrying a crate. He also tugged on his thick cape, feeling the cold as he shivered. "Why are we wasting our time to help the pilot fill his pockets?"

Kora gave Tarak a side glance. "You're with us because of him. If we're going to stand a chance, we have to start trusting each other."

Tarak watched Kai talk to a dockworker chewing on a hemp twig. "Doesn't mean I have to like him. Not after the other night. Don't mind me if I keep an eye on him."

"Didn't say anything about liking him." Kora stopped. Her face dropped as her eyes followed a face that didn't belong. Her mind cast back to Providence. One of the Hawkshaws caught her eye because of a large thick scar running down the side of his face. The same scar that she saw now. When he looked the other way, she dropped her crate and swung around to Tarak. She looked directly into his eyes and grabbed his wrist. Her voice was low. "This isn't right." She looked to Kai, who held her gaze and smiled. In that instant, she *knew*.

A large explosion boomed above their heads. Shrapnel and fire rained down on the docks as one of Bloodaxe's ships was incinerated. Kora and the others reached for their weapons as they searched the sky for an attacking ship. Dockworkers scrambled for cover, screaming obscenities over each other. There was nothing in the crew's immediate eyesight.

"Get ready for a fight!" shouted Darrian in the distance as he frantically searched for the source of the chaos. One of his fighter ships began firing. In an instant it burst into a ball of flame. While distracted by burning falling debris, the warriors didn't notice metal hitting metal and the clinking of gears. The warriors looked around, poised to fight an enemy still unseen. The silver crates they had unloaded creaked opened. Metal began to unfold and twist with origami precision until it formed a hulking exoskeleton.

In seconds the robotic jailer had Kora's neck, waist, and arms in vise-like shackles. Before the others could react, they were detained with the same speed and in the same fashion. Nemesis twisted her arms to free herself, but the more she resisted, the tighter it gripped. Her swords clattered to the ground as the pressure points in her metal wrists were squeezed. She gritted her teeth. Though she didn't cry out, she begrudgingly accepted her defeat and stopped her futile writhing. Kora couldn't look at any of them. This was her fault. But where had they screwed up?

"Kora!" screamed Gunnar, who was still free. He was with Darrian's fighters, who were not detained. The fighters reached for their weapons, but they were a day late and a dollar short. Kai and the Hawkshaw bounty hunters had weapons pointed at them before they could even draw. Gunnar and the Bloodaxe crew had no choice but to surrender.

Kai strutted around the detainees with a smirk, then stopped in front of Kora. She gave him a glare of murderous rage, though she felt a million emotions. She couldn't help but be reminded of the first monumental betrayal in her life. "You fucking piece of shit. When?"

"I knew he was a lying asshole!" shouted Tarak as he flexed his arms, trying to escape. Kai chortled and gave them a smug smile. He opened his mouth to speak when the entire docks rumbled like one of the eastern storms had moved in their direction. They all looked to the sky, then below them. A large launch ship rose from the dark mist surrounding the water and black-bladed rocks. Kora glanced at a still smiling Kai and back at the ship. She trembled with terror. Kai moved to catch her gaze.

"When, Kora? On Veldt, in Providence, the first time I heard your story. Thought with your ideals of resistance I could round up a couple of heads. Tarak, for instance. His world enslaved. Then there was Nemesis. Her whole family slaughtered. But General Titus? Have you any idea how much he alone is worth? They would have all jumped at the chance to exact any small vengeance against the Realm, even if the payment was only a sack of grain. Then there was you. Kora. Or should I call you Arthelais? The biggest prize of them all."

Kora continued to glare at him and turned her attention to the gunship connecting with a third dock. The doors opened and the ramp lowered. She looked back at Kai. "Your home. Was it even destroyed?"

Kai's expression turned serious. "Do you know what the Motherworld did to my planet? They didn't just destroy it. They tortured every man, woman, and child. Left them clingin' to life as they turned them to ash from low orbit. You know what that taught me? Never set foot on the wrong side of history."

"That's what you think we're doing?"

He frowned and shook his head. "No. You've chosen the side that doesn't even make it to the history books."

The sound of heavy footfalls on metal turned everyone's attention to the launch ship. Noble led the way with bone scepter in hand and a sword on his belt. His Krypteian Guards, Balbus and Felix, behind him. Kora turned her attention back to Kai. "What happened to honor?"

"What did happen to it?" he said.

Noble sized up all the warriors with his head held high. He stopped in front of Darrian first. "Well, who all have we got here? Who indeed. Commander Bloodaxe. Leader of the very insurgency *The King's Gaze* were sent to this backwater of the galaxy to capture. He alone will secure my seat in the Senate."

Darrian's nostrils flared and eyes narrowed. "Atticus Noble. You will not leave this moon alive."

Noble tapped the scepter against the machine holding Darrian hostage. "Interesting threat... From a man in shackles. You never give up hope, even when it is futile. You die now, your sister will perish soon enough."

Darrian jerked his body in the tight exoskeleton shackles to no avail. Noble chuckled before he continued to walk through the warriors. He stopped in front of Tarak. He bowed slightly. "And I would be remiss if I failed to mention we are in the presence of royalty. Tarak Decimus. Or should I say Prince Tarak?"

Tarak remained still and stoic but spat next to Noble's feet. Noble looked down before he walked on to the next prisoner. "General Titus. He needs no introduction, does he? His actions at the Battle of Sarawu precede him."

"Move on. The Imperium stench on your breath makes me sick," boomed Titus.

Noble gave Titus a scowl. "The feeling is mutual." He continued on, and faced Nemesis. Her eyes glowered with animosity and her metal hands shook.

"The legendary swordswoman known only by the name of Nemesis. Assassinated sixteen high-ranking Imperial officers and their security detail. All in a hunt to avenge her slaughtered children. Of course."

Nemesis growled, "Don't you dare speak of them. Their names, all the dead's names, deserve better than your mouth."

"I don't even know their names," he said matter-of-factly.

One of the Hawkshaws kicked the fallen sword to her right. "Blades of oracle steel… Been searching for one of these for ages. How do you get 'em glow?" He leaned down to have a closer look.

Nemesis craned her neck to see what he was about to do. "I will rip them from your hands and use them to cleave your head from your body. Then they will glow orange with the fires of the forge of Byeol."

The Hawkshaw grunted and scooped up one of the blades from the ground, placing it under his belt. "Mine now." Her eyes followed him with sizzling hatred as he walked away.

Noble scanned the group until he caught sight of Gunnar. He walked toward him slowly. "The farmer. The ambitious farmer. I pride myself on never being surprised. And yet, here I am. I understand why all of them are here but you. What could you have possibly hoped to gain by mounting such a… feeble stand? Tell me. This?"

"Because I stand for something beyond coercion, murder, and hate."

Noble scrunched his face in a mocking gesture. "How stupid." He patted Gunnar's left cheek, followed by a hard slap.

"Enough games, Noble," Kora said.

He stepped toward her. His eyes slithered over her body as he stood inches from her. He took her gun from the holster and tossed it to the ground. "And I thought I recognized something in you, down in that filthy village. But here, amongst all these simple people, the most wanted fugitive in the known universe. Scargiver, Arthelais."

"That isn't my real name. That is not who I am," said Kora.

Noble dismissed her with a wave. "Do you realize,

truly, Arthelais, what you have done for me, assembling yourselves as such? When I lay your paralyzed bodies at the regent's feet, I will be a hero of the Realm. They will write songs of my feats of courage."

Kai cleared his throat and looked off. "It's not like I didn't do all the work," he said under his breath.

Noble shot Kai a look, devoid of anger or surprise, devoid of anything. The eyes are the windows to the soul, and it was then Kai saw that Noble didn't have one. He backed down without saying another word.

"Let's move this along, shall we?" said Noble.

Kai gave him a nod and unclipped a bolt gun from one of the unopened silver crates that matched the ones that held Kora and the warriors. He held it up and inspected the barrel and projectile inside. "Let's transport them paralyzed, in case anyone's feeling frisky. Just one shot to sever the spine is all it takes with this bad boy." He pointed it at Gunnar and pulled the trigger. The coupling ring and paralysis spike ejected and retracted. He walked toward Gunnar, then offered it to him. "On your feet. I've got a job for you. You play your cards right, you at least might make it out of this alive."

Gunnar didn't move. He swallowed hard and looked at the warriors staring at him, waiting to see what he would do.

Noble glanced at Kai, then back at Gunnar. "He's not going to be a problem?"

Kai threw his head back and laughed. "First time I met him—a gunfight—you know what he does? Scampers under her legs, cowers behind her while she does the dirty work. He's a coward."

Gunnar looked down, unsure which point to argue. Unsure which was untrue. He looked back at the bolt gun in Kai's hand. He snatched it away. Kai cocked his head toward Kora. Gunnar shook his head, on the verge of tears.

Kai smirked and turned to Noble. "This is what I call entertainment. He's in love with her. The way he moons over her when he thinks she isn't watching. It's pathetic. He hasn't made a move this entire time and I would bet my ship he never would have either. No balls for love or war."

Gunnar faced Kora. Their eyes met. "Gunnar... If you do this... They will still kill you. At least die with honor."

He walked around behind Kora. His hand trembled as he placed the bolt gun into the coupling chamber. Kai took three large strides until he was next to Gunnar. "Don't be a pussy. Do it. A woman like her would never love a man like you. I'm doing you a favor really. Kora's brave, ferocious, powerful, y'know? You're... you."

Gunnar leaned closer to her, ignoring Kai and everyone around them. "I'm sorry," said Gunnar as he looked at the screen that showed an image of her spine. He clenched his jaw and twisted the bolt gun ninety degrees. In an instant, a series of clicks shattered the silence. The steel jaws holding Kora released her. Without missing a beat, she sprinted forward into action, toward one of the heavily armed Hawkshaws.

Gunnar withdrew the bolt gun and thrust it beneath Kai's chin. "I'm brave enough to die for something." Their eyes met in the moment he pulled the trigger, realization in Kai's eyes, steely determination in Gunnar's. The spike shot straight through Kai's skull. His eyes rolled from black to solid white as blood gushed from his nostrils, falling into his open mouth. Gunnar pulled out the bolt gun as Kai's corpse dropped limply to the floor. He rushed toward Nemesis and released her. Gunfire, aimed at him from newly emerged soldiers and Noble, made him duck for cover behind the crates. Nemesis dropped to her feet and grabbed her sword from the ground. It glowed red as soon as it touched her hand. She moved to the confined warriors and swiped a sword against the coupling ring at the back of the collar.

As the Hawkshaws prepared to take down a charging Kora, Darrian's fighters took advantage of the ensuing chaos. They shouted their battle cries before attacking the Hawkshaws, quicker to jump on the man closest to them than drawing their guns. In seconds it became a frantic and confused brawl. Kora attacked the Hawkshaw nearest to her, disarming him in one movement and killing him in the next. She aimed the weapon toward a fuel tank at the edge of the dock and fired. The explosion made everyone duck, dockworkers scrambled for cover as the fire blazed through the darkness of night.

Nemesis whipped her head around until she laid eyes on the Hawkshaw who had her other sword. She charged toward him. When he raised his rifle at her, she dropped to her knees and slid toward him, grabbing her missing sword from the side of his belt. She sliced across his waist. The leather cut with the smoothness of butter and so did

REBEL MOON

231

his body. His torso and the bottom half fell in separate directions. She wasted no time, dodging and deflecting bullets with her steel to help Tarak out of his cage. She cut the back of the exoskeleton to release him, her swords glowing with hellfire born from vengeance.

Titus was the last to be freed. More gunfire bounced off her blades as she tried to get to him. Titus breathed heavily and balled his fists ready for the fight. With a short break from being a target as Tarak began his own attack against their enemies, she cracked open Titus's exoskeleton cage. As he fell to the ground, she raised her sword inches from his face. His eyes went wide with a bright orange spear reflecting in his pupils. A loud *ping* against her sword was followed by a scream in the distance from a Hawkshaw being hit by the ricochet. She looked past her sword, which had acted as a shield, and into his eyes. "I owe you one," he said.

She gave him a nod and cocked her head toward the fray, where Tarak had taken control of another Hawkshaw weapon. This one, easily the size of two men's arms, was known for its rapid fire of bone-shattering bullets. His muscled arms held it high enough to spray the approaching soldiers and Hawkshaws. Kora used this opportunity to dodge between bodies and crates. She positioned herself behind one with her weapon aimed at the unsuspecting soldiers. With elite precision she cut them down like rotting branches weighing down a tree. Her crosshairs moved until they landed on the one man she knew had to die at all costs: Noble. She wanted to do it.

He was on his own, his Krypteian guards were picking up the Hawkshaws' slack. Her finger pressed and she held her breath until it blasted through the neck of a Hawkshaw. "*Fuck!*" she said under her breath. The whirring of a ship distracted her. Noble's craft rose from the dock with its guns coming alive. Her eyes darted to the fight on the ground. She knew what would come next, and she wasn't the only one to notice.

Darrian whipped his head around the battle, surveying who was left. He returned his attention to the rising ship. "Pilots! To your ships!" he shouted to his remaining fighters and pointed to the ships. They all charged toward the dock, where their ships were tethered together.

Kora silently watched their backs, picking off anyone who tried to interfere with their dash to the ships. But it was not enough. Noble's ship hovered over Darrian's crew as they began to launch and fired indiscriminately. Darrian was blown back by the impact of the explosion of his ships. Out of instinct, his arms raised to shield his face. When he lowered them again, he let out a bloodcurdling scream with his arms lifted at his sides. His thick neck bulged with veins as he continued to cry out in fury. He was no longer just a rebel; in that moment, he was all warrior from Shasu.

Tarak rushed to his side with his automatic weapon firing at Noble's ship and the soldiers. A wave of torn flesh and blood burst into the air. Titus scooped up a dropped Hawkshaw automatic and stood wide-legged next to Tarak. The two men caught each other's eye and exchanged wicked smiles while they mowed down soldiers of the Realm with the same amount of mercy the Realm had extended to them. The same mercy the Motherworld had for the universe in its all-consuming appetite for devouring others. The warriors expelled all their hate for the Realm in smoke and metal.

Kora remained in her hiding spot. With Tarak and Titus firing heavy artillery, she hunted for Noble again. "*Goddammit!*" she whispered to herself once she'd spotted him. Noble's men were pulling him away and shielding instant kill points on his body, despite his protests. That man loved the kill and chaos of conquest. He couldn't just be wounded or scared. He had to go down for good. She still attempted to kill as many of the bastards around him as she could, but decided to swing back to Titus, Darrian, and Tarak to keep the heat off them. She could hear Nemesis fighting in the distance, the ugly sounds and scrapes of metal on metal and the howls of agony from the soldiers she encountered.

Nemesis wielded her swords with the grace and beauty of a large bird of prey soaring freely through a valley. Soldiers and Hawkshaws fell in her wake.

"You!" screamed the Krypteian Guard, Felix. He began to fire in her direction. Nemesis welcomed the game and deflected his shots with her own blades still hot. Blood and hair from slain enemies sizzled on their heat. When his weapon was spent, he tossed it to the side and grunted, baring his yellowed teeth. He caught her blade with his own. Sparks showered between them, reflecting in their eyes as they met nose to nose. Felix pushed back to get a clean swipe, but Nemesis caught his blow, taking a sliver of his blade. He growled and charged at her again with increased speed. He raised his oversized shoulder to hit her hard. It only served for her to cut even more off his blade. He stumbled back from the energy shift coming off their swords. Nemesis pushed forward, each thrust of her sword angrier and faster than the last. Sparks and large pieces of his blade flew into the air.

With his sword's jagged stump, he punched the side of her arm. It pushed her off balance. As she regained her footing, he rushed toward her and swung at her again, hitting her on the temple. The impact made her fall to the ground. Before she could blink to catch her bearings, he was on her. He straddled her, lifting the remnants of his sword into the air. With his nostrils flared, his eyes wild with humiliation and vengeance, and spittle dribbling onto the stubble around his mouth, Nemesis could only see the Krypteian as an animal. She knew she would die by the sword, but not today, not to this beast.

"I'm gonna stick you so hard, bitch. If we were alone… what I would do to you…"

Nemesis knew her sword was close, she could feel its heat. It was an extension of the wrath in her soul, the flames that kept her going beyond grief. With her left hand, she gripped the handle and swung it across Felix's shoulders. Blood spurted in thin streams like tendrils into the air. She bucked her hips so his body would fall to the side, not on top of her. She stood above him and put the back of her heel into his skull. For a second, she was annoyed that she had been bested, if only briefly.

"Cover me! Noble's getting away!" shouted Kora. Nemesis looked up and gave her a nod.

Kora dashed from her lookout spot to catch up to a retreating Noble. His ship continued to shoot while on the move, but rotated around a crane. On her flank she saw Darrian running past her with Milius close behind, covering him from the onslaught of firepower. He ran straight for the crane near the enemy ship without hesitation. As he climbed the stairs, the ship fired, hitting him in the left shoulder. The blow made him stumble back with a loud shout and curse, but his steely gaze remained fixed on the ship. As he climbed further, he grabbed a thin fallen piece of shrapnel that resembled a spear. He continued to rush up the stairs until he was close enough to make a giant leap of faith, arms and legs spread wide and metal in hand.

Kora thought he'd missed, but he just about landed on the nose of the ship with his fingers dug into a seam. The vessel careened as the pilot tried to shake him off. His knuckles went white, holding on and trying to keep his balance. One of his feet slipped until he regained its grip. Darrian's right hand plunged the blade into the metal of the ship. He climbed higher onto the nose and pulled the blade out to break the windshield. In an expulsion of glass, he nearly stabbed the pilot. The ship teetered, with the pilot caught off guard and losing control. He pulled out a pistol with one hand to shoot a crazed Darrian, high on adrenaline and fury. The shot went through Darrian's chest.

His eyes fluttered, but it wasn't enough to stop him. He continued to climb up the ship. The shaky pilot's hand shot again, managing to graze his forearm this time, only to incite more rage in Darrian. "If I am going to die, so will you!" he screamed as blood poured from his wound.

He climbed close enough to the cockpit to press his shrapnel spear into the pilot's chest, killing him in an instant. The ship rocked and began to spiral with firepower blasting the sides of the ship. The control panel continued to blink red, the hits were shutting it down. Darrian took the controls in hand and held on, as there was no direction to go other than the surface of Gondival. He continued to shake his head to stay alert as his life began to fade, his body shutting down like the hunk of metal he clung to. "Death to the Motherworld! Death to the Realm! For Shasu!" he shouted with hysterical laughter as he allowed the ship to fall in the name of liberty.

Kora ran through the chaos to catch Noble, who had been separated from the last of his men. The weapon she had previously fired was out of ammunition, so she tossed it to the ground. Her intention was to kill Noble one way or another, even if it had to be with her bare hands. The mist and wind whipped more violently around her. Fighting could still be heard in the distance. One of the burning ships approached the docks as it fell from the sky. Kora ran harder and slid beneath it before it could separate her from Noble. As she rushed toward Noble, he turned quickly to face her. In his arrogance he raised his chin slightly.

"I'm going to enjoy this, *Arthelais*. And just wait until Balisarius sees your dead body," he said, raising the bone scepter in one hand. In that instant he looked like a monster revealing its lethal jaws and teeth, anxious for a kill. Kora knew the only way to stop men like Noble and Balisarius was through death. Their endless hunger for power and destruction only grew the more they accumulated.

She had been trained the same way as Noble and this was to her advantage. His every move would be calculated with precision. They both bolted forward at the same time for the first blow. He swung for her head with the bone staff. She ducked before impact then bounced back up and backed away to a safe distance.

"I'm surprised, Noble. I thought murder would have grown old for you. You are a master of it, after all."

"Says the murderer."

A sudden deafening screech of crunching metal and shouts filled the atmosphere. Both jerked their heads toward the noise, then dove out of the way of the gunship crashing into a floating dock. Kora could just see the outline of a man hanging onto the nose before turning back to Noble, who was back on his feet, charging toward her. He managed to hit her in the ribs with his staff. She doubled over but kept her eyes on him. As she held her waist, she charged forward to headbutt him in the stomach. The blow caught him off guard; however, he took hold of her, causing them both to fall to the ground. Kora screamed between gritted teeth, trying to land enough punches and kicks to disable him. He fought just as hard, with hate in his eyes.

Kora could hear the water crashing against the jagged teeth of rocks below and feel the wind picking up around them. She glanced to her left. They were close to the edge. There was no way he could survive a fall like that. The thought gave her renewed determination and strength. She fought harder to get him closer to the edge of the dock. He looked at the edge and thought the same. He tumbled on top of her and placed the staff horizontally over her neck. His eyes glared into hers as he pressed it into her throat. He smiled as he watched her struggle beneath his weight.

There was no way his vile face would be the last thing she saw before dying. She grabbed both ends of the staff and twisted him to the left. At the same time, she swung her dangling leg around his waist and pulled them both over the edge. She could feel the rush of cold wind embrace her. They fell from the dock, and instead of the boulders, they landed hard on a floating octagonal buoy ten feet below. Both scrambled to their feet. Noble grabbed his staff from nearby, which had fallen with them. Kora charged forward, landing punches to his face. He returned each hit. Both of their faces were soon bloody. Noble swung the bone toward her temple, but she ducked and scrambled to the side.

"All you do is run. I will drag your dead body back for my glory. Glory that is long overdue," he sneered.

Kora crouched slightly and moved with slow steps and arms spread at her sides, trying to anticipate his next move. "You do the same, running from planet to planet, but you only bring death and terror. I will leave your dead body where it falls. You don't deserve any better in this life."

His eyes narrowed before swinging the scepter at her legs. Kora fell and tumbled to the edge of the buoy. Before falling to the rocks below, she caught a hanging rope. Her feet dangled in the cold wind as she climbed up. Noble raised his scepter and smashed it against the rope, severing it from the buoy, but it was not quick enough for Kora to have already held fast to the metal ledge. She pulled herself up and grabbed the remaining piece of the rope and began to swing it at him. She caught him in the chest and legs. She grabbed his arm holding the scepter and twisted it until he screamed from his radius cracking and piercing through his skin. Kora used the moment to break the scepter in two, using one half to spear his thigh.

Noble stumbled back, weaponless. The large shard of the scepter remained in her hands. His eyes were comets of rage as he stepped back. Kora swung it hard, hoping he felt some semblance of fear. They held each other's gaze as she stepped closer, and he stepped back. He stopped and glanced behind his shoulder. His hair blew in the wind. He stood at the edge of the small buoy, nothing but churning dark water with lethal undertows and rocks below their feet.

Kora looked at the staff, then back to Noble. "You're out of time," she said as she lifted the scepter.

He smiled and sneered. "What is time? What is memory or love, or loyalty? The Imperium is all these things. It is all-encompassing and can never be defeated. You and those *rebels* have no hope and soon will be out of time. There is nowhere in this universe you won't be found."

She brought up the bone, held like a spear at shoulder height, and hurled it hard toward him. His eyes dropped to his chest, his lips parted. The staff protruded from the center of his sternum. Blood trickled from the corners of his mouth as he looked over his shoulder with nowhere to go, then back at Kora with a look of bewilderment.

Kora walked toward him with calm steps. His hands gripped the staff as if he wanted to pull it out. She lifted her foot and kicked him over the edge without saying a word. To be sure of his demise, she watched him fall until his body slammed into the exposed obsidian rocks. His shattered arms and legs took on an unnatural shape. Blood trailed behind him like cape into the salt water. The incoming tide swirled around the base of the rocky ledge where he lay with the limpness of loose seaweed.

Part of her wished it was Balisarius who lay dead. If anyone truly deserved death, it was him. He who had twisted her loyalty and manipulated her broken heart. She would probably never get the chance to face him. To say all that went left unsaid. Now that she had time to process her years with him and the day she fled, she would never know why he did what he did. The past roiled and crashed in Kora's mind like the waves below.

Satisfied seeing him unmoving, Kora looked toward the docks, hoping someone would come to her aid soon with the fighting done. She waved her hands above her head when she saw Tarak and Milius surveying the damage and possibly looking for survivors. Tarak pointed to her, and shouted, "Hold tight!"

She stood on the buoy alone now, feeling the cold. It was over, but for how long? She wondered what was happening on Veldt and if she could consider going back, for good. It was a wonderful dream. She remembered Kai's words about Gunnar. Her heart ached, thinking about when he saved her. She didn't need saving, nor would she ever ask for it. But it was nice to know there was one person out there who would stick their neck out for her.

A rope tied with a monkey-paw knot dropped near her feet and caught on the railing of the buoy. She looked up to see Tark pulling on the rope, lifting the buoy toward the docks. As it rose, Gunnar stood just behind him, guiding the rope as well. His silhouette highlighted by the fires of battle. His face and clothing were blood-spattered. They locked eyes as she stepped off the buoy and back onto the dock. There was a softness, a sense of relief inside her that made her want to run to him, but that was not her way. She never had any arms to fall into. She nodded at him.

"You did it," he said as he faced her, standing close.

She glanced over his shoulder toward the metal exoskeleton cages. "So did you. Thank you."

"Some things are worth dying for." His eyes didn't waver or stray as he said this. She could feel his breath on her cheek and his body close enough that all she had to do was lift a hand to touch him. His lips not much farther.

Titus joined them, followed by the rest of the warriors, breaking the moment. Gunnar took a step back and pulled Kora's weapon from the back of his belt. "Found this. Thought you might want it back."

She smiled and took it into her hands.

Titus's posture was straight, his head held high as he looked over the destruction and dead soldiers. "This was a blow to the Motherworld, what we did this day. Criminals, nobodies, standing against a machine of war. This small act of defiance gives voice to the voiceless. This is more than just a fallen prick officer and some of his men. It's the beginning of something."

Kora listened intently to Titus. "The beginning of what?"

He shook his head and looked to the sky. "I don't know yet. Something strong."

He gave her a wide grin before pulling out his flask and taking a long gulp. He passed it to Tarak, who drank in solidarity.

"You think they will retaliate? What will they do now?" asked Nemesis.

Kora surveyed the docks. "Undercrews of the Imperium are not known for their bravery. After the death of an admiral, protocol will demand the ship's return."

"That's good," Gunnar said.

"We still get paid, I presume?" asked Titus.

"A deal is a deal. Payment awaits us on Veldt," Kora said.

Tarak slapped Gunnar on the back and smiled. "I owe you thanks, Gunnar. You know, I never did trust that pilot."

Kora glanced at Gunnar. "We all owe him thanks. He saved us."

Titus raised his flask. "Three cheers for Gunnar."

Gunnar blushed as they started the chorus. "Why don't we get out of here and head back to Veldt. Anyone know how to fly that thing?" he said to change the subject, as he pointed to Kai's intact ship. Kora nodded and smiled while the others continued to chuckle at his expense.

Aris was happy not to be sleeping in the granary, but he still had to keep any eye on the transmissions. They needed as much time as possible for Kora and Gunnar to return before Noble. Sam kindly allowed him to stay in the front room of the small home she'd inherited from her mother. Before entering, she stopped in front of the door. Her hand rested on the handle. "It's probably not as nice as what you are used to. But it's warm and comfortable. I was born here. The village has come together to help me maintain it over the years. It's all I have left of my family, so I try to keep it in the best condition I can."

"I'm sure it's fine."

Sam opened the door. The bedroom and main room were separated by a short wall made from wood. On one side her bed, and on the other a small square table with two chairs. An empty glass milk bottle had wildflowers inside. The large window behind the table allowed light to flood in. She had a basic kitchen for cooking, with a hearth next to it. His eyes scanned the walls and bed. There were beautiful quilts hanging on the walls and one lay over the bed. It was of the landscape surrounding the village. Sam noticed him smiling as he looked at them. "When not helping out in the fields, I make things. I love sewing and quilting."

"They are fantastic. Where did you learn to do this?"

"My grandmother. She taught me when I was old enough to hold a needle and thread. After my mother left, this is what I did to pass the time and heal from missing her. Whenever anyone needs a new blanket, I make them one."

"You are very talented."

The young woman blushed. "I'm glad you like them, because you will be sleeping on them tonight. I have so many."

"Thank you, Sam. I hope I can earn my keep here." He glanced around the room. A basket with remnants of kindling wood next to the hearth was empty. "Can I get you some firewood?"

She smiled. "That would be lovely. Then we can light it and have a light supper."

When Aris returned with more wood, Sam sat at the table with bread, cheese, and a salad of sliced root vegetables. He placed the wood in the basket and sat down. "You have really made me feel at home. I can't thank you enough."

"It's the least I can do. Besides, there are a few other jobs that might need seeing to.

They both laughed while digging into the meal. As Sam tore into the bread, her expression turned serious. "Are you afraid of dying? You said you weren't really a soldier."

Aris stopped eating. "I don't want to die, but I am also not afraid. Some things are worse than death."

"Like killing?"

Aris nodded without looking at her. "Are you asking because you were afraid? There is nothing wrong with that. What those men did to you, wanted to do."

"I know. But what if I have to kill to live? There is still so much to see and experience. And depending on what happens when Kora gets back…"

Aris's eyes snapped toward her. "Please leave when they do. I will help you. Go far from here. You don't deserve war."

Sam placed a hand on his. "No one does. No one deserves brutality or having their home ripped from them. Or families torn apart. I will stay and fight with everyone else, even if it means I will die."

He smiled. "You know, you are braver than some of the soldiers I have met."

She looked away. "I don't know about that. But I do take pride in my work and living on my own from such a young age."

"When did your mother die?"

"When I was twelve."

Aris thought of his sisters and how devoted his parents were to giving them all a stable family life. His heart ached for Sam, who was kinder than the life given to her. She seemed not to possess an ounce of bitterness. Inside her was a spring that flowed from her soul and touched everything and everyone around her. It was where her courage and beauty came from. He felt grateful to know her. His family would have loved her.

"I was older, but I understand." He glanced at the unlit hearth. "How about I light that fire now?"

Sam gave him a wide grin that put him at ease in an instant. "Sure. And then we can arrange my extra quilts for your bed."

THE FREIGHTER LANDED IN PROVIDENCE AT DUSK. GUNNAR AND KORA WERE THE first off the ship. He took a deep breath and looked toward Kora. "Wow. Feels strange to be back here… and not alone. We did what we set out to do. I'm grateful to be back. And for your help."

Kora smiled. "Let's get back to the village. A good night's sleep in Hagen's house sounds great right now."

The warriors trickled out of the freighter and surveyed their surroundings. Tarak spotted the Pleasure Emporium. "Do we have time for a quick drink? One for the road?"

Titus elbowed him. "A drink? Is that all that is on your mind?"

"Hey, I've been shackled for way too long. You'd be craving a drink too."

Kora motioned to him to follow. "Sorry to disappoint, but we should get back to the village sooner rather than later. We have much to do."

Gunnar led them to the local stables and managed to get enough uraki at a fair price to travel back to the village under cover of darkness. They left Providence and rode until the sun rose above the mountains and Mara's red hue could be seen across the land. Kora rode faster than the others, giving her space to think of what might happen next. Should she remain on Veldt or was it time to move on? Her emotions were as unclear as the Gondival sky. She could hear the snorts and grunting of a uraki approaching. Titus caught up to Kora.

"Is what that dead bounty hunter said true? The name he called you? Arthelais?"

Kora didn't look at Titus. The only way she could ever lead a normal life was if the old one could die and be forgotten. Including that name. It wasn't who she was born to be. "Kai was a liar and a thief who nearly sold you all for a profit. Anything more you want, General?"

He continued to look at her, not knowing if this was the truth or not. But he left it at that. "Don't call me 'General'."

Kora nodded and rode on past Titus until they reached the end of the dusty mountain road, before it descended to make its way to the village. From that spot the entire valley could be seen, surrounded by more snow-capped mountains and lush forest-covered hills, with a pristine river snaking in the center. Mara rose from behind it, giving the morning mist a reddish hue that melted into pale yellow from the rising sun. Kora wouldn't say it out loud because it wasn't her way, but part of her felt a sense of calm, seeing the village still standing.

She had never felt that a place would create a deep yearning inside her again since she was a child, and found herself on an Imperium ship being told she would never see her home world again. For years she had seen many worlds decimated. It would devastate her to see this village levelled to nothing and the people she had grown to know tortured and dead.

"That's our village. That's home." Gunnar was beside her with a smile on his face, a sense of pride in his posture and in his eyes as he gazed at the tiny village. He looked how she felt inside.

"Home. I never had a place to put to the word," she said to him. His hand moved to touch hers, but he pulled back.

Tarak stopped next to them, taking in the breathtaking landscape. "It's almost a shame you killed that bastard Noble and that we don't have to fight. This would have been a beautiful place to die."

Kora smiled and inhaled the brisk morning air. "Yes, it would. But maybe it is meant to be home for a while longer." She heeled the uraki at the same time as Gunnar. They began their descent into the valley.

The brush rustled above them when they were far enough away not to hear or see they had company. Two Hawkshaws moved with stealth as they followed the warriors back to the village. One of them turned to the leader. "What now?"

"We wait. We don't make any moves until we receive orders. Let's go back to the falls."

Mara Falls stood above the village and fell into a rocky pool. Its clean, cool waters came directly from the snow-capped mountains. Five hundred feet above the village were flat rock ledges carved into the side of a mountain that surrounded the village. The Hawkshaws who followed Kora and the warriors from Providence had been using this hidden spot as a base to spy on the group and the village. One of them stood at the ledge of a cliff, on watch with binoculars in hand. Two others dropped their supplies and equipment.

The thinner and smaller one of the Hawkshaws walked over to the ledge. "What news, Syra?"

He turned to his companion. "'Bout time you got back here, Streep. They all went into the longhouse. Probably eating and drinking. That will give us time to set up a transmitter. Get Kaan to find firewood. This place will do nicely while we await further instructions."

Syra turned to the other Hawkshaw unloading supplies. "You're on firewood duty."

Kaan's eyes narrowed, and he growled, "I always get the shit jobs."

"That's because you haven't earned your place yet," shouted Syra.

Kaan sulked toward the forest. He looked around the immediate area to avoid wandering too far and making this task more difficult than it had to be. The sound of a cracking tree branch made him look up. He sniffed the air, trying to detect what or who it could be. Wood deer, various birds, rotting leaves, mice. Nothing out of the ordinary.

He continued on, grabbing smaller pieces for kindling and larger ones for a longer burn. He looked up again as a tree shook with birds taking flight. He sniffed again and glanced around. He could hear the falls in the distance, but nothing else again. He looked down and kicked a snake off his boot. "I hate this place. Wish we were still in Providence," he muttered to himself, before rushing to grab any fallen branches he could find. If they wanted more, they could get it. Kaan turned from the forest to walk back into the cave behind the falls.

Jimmy rose from out of the stillness of the forest. He had hidden behind a large overturned tree. Its giant roots with packed soil and compacted leaves were the perfect shield. He had spent time in the golden fields, touching the long stalks of wheat and watching the simple beauty in nature and the healing balm of solitude. It amazed him how the wilderness possessed a perfect balance left on its own. Everything interacted in a perfectly aligned dance with each other. If only the beings on two legs could find the same harmony as the wilderness, learn from it. He also found himself learning as he observed the villagers from afar.

Being a silent guardian was much more interesting than being a war machine. Since the Hawkshaws arrived, he had stalked them and watched their movements. Something was happening, but he did not know exactly what. He made the decision to stay silent instead of alerting the village. The time might arise when he would have to, but for now he maintained his distance and would do what he could when necessary.

He moved back into the lushness of the forest, blending in and becoming one with it again. Jimmy felt alive. He had found a purpose beyond his protocol. This purpose was beyond what another programmed him to do for their sake: it was *his* will. That was what separated soul and machine. There were men who recreated themselves to mimic machine, yet Jimmy had transformed himself to be more than both.

DEVRA BLOODAXE LEFT SHARAAN WITH THE FEELING THAT PART OF HER
remained on the planet. There was a hollowness, similar
to when she left Shasu. Up until now she'd had her
brother by her side. In the past, they'd had their battles
with their families, with each other, with themselves.
Devra and Darrian didn't want to move forward without
agreeing on a direction, and although they'd agreed to
support their cause in different ways, it didn't feel right.

What if she never saw him again? Both their parents
were gone. Despite considering her fighters family, he was
blood and gave her support like no other. She questioned
her decision as she touched the black string with a single
red bead tied around her wrist. It was a gift from her
brother when they were children.

She couldn't think about the possibility of his death.
They had to move fast, to a destination unknown. Speed
and stealth was how they had survived until now. They

moved like the fanged creatures in the jungles of Shasu. They struck like the great ancestral hunters of their mother's tribe. Devra welled up with pride when she thought of her Shasu ancestry. She dug deep to feel comfort and strength. She needed it now more than ever as she stood alone on her ship. They might run out of allies they could trust. If the Imperium had its way, there would be no worlds to run to. There would only be the Motherworld, they wanted to dictate everything in the known universe. The price of dissent would be too high for anyone to take a real stand against them anymore.

"Devra." She turned to see a worried Omari approaching. "Do you have a destination in mind? We are flying blind right now and I'm getting questions from the others."

She shook her head. "Not yet. Still processing Darrian isn't here. But we need to regroup."

"I know. We will all miss him, but I suggest we decide soon. I received an encrypted transmission: large ships are approaching Sharaan. Before I could respond, it went dead."

"Whose ships?"

"Unclear, but I think it's safe to assume it's the Imperium. They will stop at nothing to find us."

Devra closed her eyes and took a deep breath. "I pray King Levitica is prepared. He is a good leader and helped us when no one else would."

"He knew the risk, we all do." He paused. "You have been very quiet since we left. Want to talk about it?"

She paused and stared at the place where Darrian

usually sat. She touched her bracelet again. The string and bead twirled in her fingers as she articulated what she felt in the bottom of her soul. "Did I make the right decision?"

"We should gather *all* our people and come up with a plan."

Devra nodded. "I feel like this is a turning point for me, us. But I need time to contemplate, weigh it all in front of me."

"I understand. But we live on borrowed time."

"Put out the message we are going to Base One. It's been a while since we have been there. It should be safe."

"Do you want me to verify the identity of the ships approaching Sharaan?"

"No. We can't risk any more transmissions. We stay way under the radar until I have a better idea of what happens next. If it is the Imperium, there is nothing else we can do now."

"I will make sure everyone knows about the new rendezvous point."

"Thank you, Omari. I just need a moment alone."

Omari gave her a short nod then left. Regrouping at Base One held the least risk and could give her the space she needed to think. Sometimes she wished she possessed her brother's boldness. Other times, she recognized that it was her measured steps that had kept her alive on Shasu and up here.

. . .

The mist descended across Gondival with the temperature dropping fast and the tide rising with violent haste. A bright light sliced through the clouds. The spotlight moved like a sniffing animal searching for prey. It stopped on the body of Noble, on the verge of being consumed by the sea. The ship lowered and the belly opened. A long robotic arm dropped and scooped up his body. It retracted with Noble's limp limbs and head dangling in the air until he disappeared into the ship.

Motherworld medical technicians stood over a floating gurney with Noble's body. One of the techs scanned his body. Cassius stared at the man who had acted as if he was invincible, yet there he was, very much susceptible to the things that break men. "Do what you have to do," said Cassius as he watched the two medical staff prepare Noble's body by removing his clothing. The gurney began to read his vitals and injuries as it moved with the tech and doctor, who wore red robes and ombré plastic masks with five lights attached to help with visibility during their work.

"We need to act fast. The chamber is ready." Dr Hadrian Mons jogged next to the floating gurney as it picked up speed. Noble's blueish-white skin glistened with salt water, blood still leaked from the gash in his chest.

"This will take a miracle," said Mons's tech, looking into the hole of torn flesh.

"We will see."

They turned the corner into the medical bay. The door shut automatically behind them. "Ready him for transmission. Balisarius is standing by." The doctor waved his hand across a strip of light on the side of the gurney. They placed Noble on a flat platform. The tech searched the back of Noble's head with his fingertips. "It's somewhere here… but we don't have much time." He continued to search until he pulled at the skin seam and peeled it back from the skull. Blood and strings of muscle pulled away from the bone. "Okay. Quickly now."

A tech pulled down on the hanging cables and plugged them into bloody ports at the base of Noble's skull with the sound of a vacuum. "Show me vitals," said the doctor loudly into the room. A hologram of Noble's body and his organs flashed above the gurney. It stopped on the still heart. "Full energy. Send him now."

Liquid began to rise around Noble. Electric-blue bolts zapped from the bottom of the tank. Noble's body convulsed with the surge of energy. The hologram of his heart pumped erratically three times then flatlined. His limp body continued to float.

"Hope he was ready to die," said one of the techs.

Mons stared sharply at Noble's body. "Men like him are always ready. That is why they are so hard to kill."

"You're not saying… There can't be anything going on in there."

Dr Mons remained silent, looking for any slight movement as data scrolled next to the hologram of Noble's heart. "Maybe not, but we have our orders. The Regent is waiting to speak to him, so we will know soon enough if he makes it."

The liquid rising around Noble's body formed an

amniotic sac that rose above the platform. He was entirely encased as he curled into the fetal position. Blue streaks of electricity crackled around him as the medical team and Cassius waited and watched.

He couldn't feel the cold burrow into his lungs when he inhaled. Noble looked below his feet. Giant koi fish the size of two men swam beneath the ice. They snapped at one another and tumbled in the frigid water below. He stood in the winter gardens of the royal palace. The palace a dark shadow in the distance. He stretched his arms out then touched his chest. His black dress uniform looked impeccable.

He was not alone. His eyes traced a koi swimming away toward a figure standing before him. Out of instinct, Noble straightened his posture. A tall man wearing a thick coat that fell to the ice, with a cane fashioned in the same manner as the bone scepter, stood with his back turned to him. It could only be one person.

"My Lord, it is an honor to be in your presence, as always."

Balisarius turned toward him. His face hard from war but kept young with fortune and science. "How does that cold air feel in your lungs, hmmm?" He lifted his cane just above the ice and set it down with a small *click*. A thin blue line of electricity jolted from the tip.

Noble's right index finger twitched. "Balisarius. Why am I here?"

"When I learned of what happened… that the account seemed to suggest a series of events that stretched credibility… I felt it was best to get the story from you." Balisarius took one step closer. "Now tell me what was done."

Noble kept his chin held high. "I have found her. The hated other who murdered in cold blood that which we held most dear. To say her name brings a feeling of rage to my throat. I have found Arthelais."

Balisarius remained emotionless. "You're certain it's her?"

"I am, my Lord. She was in the company of the disgraced General Titus and Darrien Bloodaxe. But we are close to capturing them. Our world will unite in celebration, not only for the destruction of this pitiful insurgency, but for the bringing to justice of that ethnic impurity, the monster, the Scargiver, the enemy of us all."

Remaining as stoic as the castle behind him and as cold as the falling snow covering their shoulders, Balisarius tapped on the ice with his cane again. But this time harder. A web of cracks scuttled from beneath the point of contact.

Noble looked down at the crevasse pointing directly at him like an accusatory finger. "Your Grace…"

"And this news is meant to bring me joy? Tell me, commander, should I be showering praise upon you and the promise of glory?"

Noble tried to remain composed. "I thought…"

Another strike of Balisarius's cane sent more blue electricity through the ice. His eyes flashed with rage and his mouth twisted to a sneer.

"Thought what?! That Arthelais, the assassin of the royal family, she who killed the king and queen as well as her charge, the Princess Issa, in cold blood, one of the most dangerous and decorated warriors in the history of armed conflict is now part of a blossoming insurgency? I'm supposed to be happy that she has joined forces with the genius battlefield commander, General Titus? Did you think that would be good news?"

"Sir, she is within our grasp. Let me bring you her head."

Balisarius struck the ice hard as he gripped the top of the gilded bone. More claws of broken ice reached for Noble.

"In truth, I fear the head most endangered here is yours. You will crush this insurgency to the last man, do you hear me? And then you will capture my daughter alive and bring back my precious child to me."

Noble was silent.

"So that I may crucify her in the shadow of the Senate. If you cannot bring her to me, then the one whose public execution will send shivers down the spines of the senators, and whose screams will echo down its marbled halls... will be yours." Balisarius lifted his cane once more, placing one hand over the other and plunged it toward the ice. A bolt of blue electricity zigzagged in sparks before bursting the ice below Noble's feet. He fell through silently.

The amniotic sac burst, leaving Noble naked and dripping wet on the metal grating of the platform. "Another burst."

The tech nodded and manually used a fob to electrify the cables directly connected to Noble. The dead man's body convulsed and twisted from the shock of energy. Both Mons and the tech looked toward the hologram. The warning continued with a numbered countdown.

"Hit him with everything."

The tech glanced at the body, then at the doctor. "But it could…"

"If you value your life and your job then do it! This comes from orders over me."

The tech pursed his lips and slid his thumb across the fob. The hologram continued to count down. Noble's body spasmed, with his back arching to an unnatural shape. His eyes opened and bulged out of their sockets. Without any screams, his mouth yawned painfully wide. The hologram blinked blue. The sound of a heartbeat was all that could be heard in the low amber light until he began to scream. The deafening noise filled the room.

END OF PART 1

ACKNOWLEDGMENTS

I would like to acknowledge Zack Snyder for creating an incredible story and remaining so fiercely dedicated to such a fantastic project; Adam Forman who was insanely helpful with the nuts and bolts in the story; the ENTIRE crew at Titan Books who work so very hard to bring stories to life for millions of people; and Daquan Cadogan and Michael Beale for their tireless work on this project and believing in me all the way. A good book is a sum of all the people involved from start to finish. Editors are an essential part of the process.

Thank you to the ancestors who guide me every day.

ABOUT THE AUTHOR

V. CASTRO is a Mexican-American writer from San Antonio, Texas, now residing in the UK. As a full-time mother she dedicates her time to her family and writing Latinx narratives in horror, speculative fiction, and science fiction. Her most recent releases include *The Haunting of Alejandra* from Del Ray and Titan Books, *The Queen of the Cicadas* from Flame Tree Press and *Goddess of Filth* from Creature Publishing.

Connect with Violet via Instagram and X @vlatinalondon or vcastrostories.com

For more fantastic fiction, author events,
exclusive excerpts, competitions, limited editions and more

VISIT OUR WEBSITE
titanbooks.com

LIKE US ON FACEBOOK
facebook.com/titanbooks

FOLLOW US ON TWITTER AND INSTAGRAM
@TitanBooks

EMAIL US
readerfeedback@titanemail.com